GW00731959

Dark
DESTINY
BLACK HOODS MC#5

Dark Destiny

He's an inmate. She's a free spirit.

Delilah believes animals can heal anyone. But she's never come up against someone like the hardened biker who rarely speaks. With Stone Face part of her inmate rehabilitation program, she's got her work cut out for her.

Stone Face isn't there to be rehabilitated. Her program is the only way to get to the man that murdered his twin sister. The same man he has vowed to end.

That hippie woman with all the animals is getting to him, though. Her curves. Her smell. The way her laugh reminds him of a time when he wasn't shattered on the inside.

But Delilah isn't part of his mission. He doesn't have time to fall in love. He will avenge his sister, no matter who gets caught in the crossfire.

To Glen,

Thank you for supporting me throughout this entire author journey.

XOXO, Avelyn

STONEFACE

THE COP at my back grabs the handcuffs on my wrists and pulls them high, digging them into the small of my back, forcing me to bend forward. "Get moving, asshole."

I don't say a word. If this fucker hadn't left his keys in the ignition of his cruiser, we wouldn't be here right now, and here is exactly where I want to be.

"This the guy who took your car, Dolan?"

The cop yanks the cuffs even higher. My arms scream in agony, but I just chuckle, knowing Dolan isn't going to live this down, ever. His cop buddies will be riling him about this shit for decades to come.

Looking over my shoulder, I scold, "What kind of cop leaves his car running while hitting on the chick working at the 7-Eleven? Bitch didn't even look eighteen, and your boy was all over her."

Dolan whips open the door of the holding cell and shoves me inside, sending me sprawling face-first onto the floor.

The shittiest part about being in handcuffs is there's no way to break your own damn fall. The instant my nose hits the concrete, I hear it crack. The pain alone tells me he broke it.

Maybe it's the dozen or so beers I'd downed tonight, or the total irony of me being manhandled by a cop while not resisting, but lying there at his feet with my face smashed against the ground, I laugh. Deep, loud, shoulder shaking laughter that comes out in spits and snorts and bubbles of blood.

"Jesus Christ, Dolan," the second officer snarls, moving to help me up. "Get a grip."

He has to use both of his hands just to get a grip around one of my biceps. He doesn't pull me up, because he wouldn't be able to if he tried, being the puny fucker he is. Though he does me a solid and balances me by tugging me upright as I get to my feet without the use of my hands.

Dolan stands in the doorway, his face contorted in anger. I can't blame him, really, seeing as I'd made him look like a fucking ass. But he also needs to know the error of his ways.

Taking a step forward, I have to bend my knees to look him straight in the eye. My laughter fades, and my face goes perfectly still. Even though I'm still flying high from the effects of my boozefest, I have no intention of letting him walk out of this cell without learning a lesson.

"You're lucky I'm such a good, law-abiding fucking citizen, 'cause I could've caused a lot of damage tonight, dickhead." The chill in my voice has Dolan's angry glare morphing into complete and total fear. "Only reason you arrested me was because I let you. Mishandling me in your care just now, though? That was a line you can't uncross."

Dolan swallows, but then narrows his eyes. "In your fucking cell, asshole."

My face doesn't change as I hold his gaze and take a step closer. I'm already going to the county lockup—I know that much—so what's one more charge to add to the list?

Rearing back, my feet planted wide, I whip my head forward and slam my forehead straight into his nose. *They don't call me StoneFace for nothing*. He drops in an instant, his hands cupping his face as he screams in agony.

I'd heard the *pop* of cartilage breaking when my forehead connected. But when he moves his hands to the side, I give a satisfying grin, ignoring the taste of blood staining my teeth. If my nose was busted, I'd say his had just been destroyed.

Still smiling wide, I lift my leg and step over Dolan, where he lies on the floor, curled on his side in the fetal position. Without a word, I walk into the cell.

"You motherfucker!" Dolan roars. "You broke my fucking nose!"

Using my foot, I slide the door to my cell shut. The clang rattles not only the bars on my cell, but the ones all the way down the row, echoing through the hallway.

"And now we're even," I snort.

He's still on the floor when I turn away, but I'm done with Dolan and his need to express dominance over me. The guy's a fucking pansy, and now he's a fucking pansy with a fucked-up nose.

I hear the second officer help Dolan to his feet, as well as their conversation, but I'm not really listening. I'm done with those pricks, anyway. Their useless little jail cell is only temporary.

After I go in front of the judge tomorrow, I'll be heading to county, and that's when the real fun will begin.

DELILAH

CALL AFTER CALL, after call. That's all I've done today, field phone calls. From the moment I woke up, until I landed in my office after doing food and water checks on the kennels, I haven't stopped working. Running a not-for-profit private animal rescue will do that to you. If you'd told me after all those years at college, studying to be a physical therapist, that this is where I would end up, I'd have laughed in your face. But even with days like today, I wouldn't give it up for the world.

Well, until Ashley sheepishly pops her head through the door of my office with a single white piece of paper in her hand and sorrow in her eyes.

"I'm sorry, Delilah. I have to put in my notice." She slides the piece of paper onto my desk, but I don't even look at it—I can't. If I do, it'll make this real.

"You're quitting?" I clarify, my voice almost trembling.

"I love volunteering here, but I'm moving to Dallas with Rick," she informs me, grimacing. "Rick proposed last night and asked me to go with him. Friday has to be my last day. I know it's not a full two weeks' notice, but I *am* a volunteer."

"He proposed? That seems sudden." She barely knows the guy, or so I thought. They'd met online maybe three months ago. He was fresh off his second divorce after leaving the military, and she had decided to dip her toes back into the dating pool after a few years of the single life. If you ask me, this decision has "disaster" written all over it. But it's her life, not mine.

Ashley slides her left hand forward, and sure enough, there's a giant diamond sparkler on her ring finger. Giant isn't really the appropriate word to describe the behemoth rock, though. Rick was definitely going for the "shock and awe" factor with her ring.

"I'm so happy for you," I lie, forcing a smile on my face. Stepping forward, I pull her into a tight hug, thinking, *silly girl*. I step away, and she beams back at me.

"I know we haven't known each other very long, but I love him." Her smile dims. "I just wish I didn't have to leave Austin."

"Are you sure you can't stay for a few more weeks? Rick will need to get settled into his new job, right?"

"You know I would stay if it were possible. I love this place, love volunteering with you, but Rick really wants me to drive up with him and start house hunting. The temporary housing is only available for a month, tops, so we're going to have to find something fast. I know this is going to leave you shorthanded, but I really have to go."

Shorthanded is an understatement, but that's how it goes when you can only offer volunteer positions. People weren't lining up for long hours and zero pay these days. With our expanding prison program, it was like searching for a needle in a haystack to find someone willing to spend a couple hours a week working directly with the animals and the inmates. Ashley is, well, *was* that needle for me. She took over the local program at the Travis County Jail after we got it started, and after a few years, we expanded into the penitentiary program, which I run. Doing both without her will be nearly impossible.

"Yeah, I know," I sigh. "But that's not a problem you need to worry about. I'll figure something out—I always do."

"Is there anything I can do to help you?"

I think quietly to myself before I answer her. "Could you maybe write up a summary about your work at the jail? The people you've been working with, and any details that you can think of for the person who will be taking over for you there."

"Of course! I can get started on that right now."

"That would be great." I pause. "I'll miss you, but I'm happy for you."

"I'll miss you too." A tear falls down her cheek, but she quickly wipes it away. "I'll go get started on that report for you." With a smile, she slips out of my office.

The second she leaves, my head drops. How am I going to do this without her? Ashley is my second-in-command, my most reliable employee, and in a few short days, she'll be leaving. I know if her position here was a paying one, she would most likely stay, but our budget barely covers the rent on our main building and the supplies for the dogs. The extra income from the jail program supplied by our local government padded it, but only slightly. Just enough to cover buying the additional van and paying for our gas. If it hadn't been for my inheritance from my late grandfather, I'd be homeless myself instead of living in my parents' old Volkswagen camper van on the rescue's property.

Shaking off the sense of dread about how I'm going to make this work, I immerse myself in the pet adoption applications I found on my desk when I came in. There were dozens for the litter of puppies that had been dumped over the weekend off the interstate, and only one for one of the older dogs. The sad state of rescues. Everyone wanted cute, cuddly puppies, and not the senior or special needs dogs who deserved to be in their forever homes too.

My ringing phone draws my attention away from the applications. Grabbing up the receiver, I greet, "Austin Animal Rescue."

"Hey, Delilah," a familiar voice replies.

"Maria, how are you doing? How's Popeye fitting in with your family?"

A few weeks ago, she and her son had come to the shelter and adopted our longest resident, Popeye, a one-eyed pit mix who needs extra care after he and four other dogs were brought to us after being used as bait dogs by a dog fighter. He was thriving here with the volunteers, but finding a home for him had been my mission over the last few years. He deserved to find his family.

"That's why I'm calling…" Her voice trails off. Oh, no. I know that tone. Not again. "Popeye's not really working out for us. We had an incident this morning."

"An incident?"

"He destroyed all of my son's toys and ripped our couch to shreds. I tried to correct him like we talked about, and he snarled at me. Tommy's scared to death of him now."

"Oh my goodness, Maria. You're both okay, right?"

"We are. He scared us more than anything, but I can't keep him."

"If you'd like me to pick him up, I can come by."

"That might be best for all of us. I'm really sorry about this. Everything was going fine until it wasn't."

"Sometimes, things don't work out." Story of the day, it seems. "Are you home now?"

"I am."

"Let me get a few things together here, and I'll come by to get him."

"I really appreciate that." She sighs in relief. "I really hate doing this, you know, but if he scares Tommy and can't behave, our landlord will kick us out of our complex if he finds out he's..." She trails off again, realizing the lie she's just let slip. "Not friendly."

"I understand," I force out, hiding the disappointment in my voice. She assured me her apartment complex was okay with him being classified as a bully breed, but clearly, she lied on her application about that. "I'll be over shortly."

"Thanks again, Delilah."

"Sure thing," I mutter. Sparks of frustration prickle beneath my skin. I wish I could say this is a one-off, but with dogs like Popeye, it happens more than I care to admit. Adopters think they'll fit right in and be a part of the family when, in fact, they need more time to adjust to their new surroundings and to create a routine of their own. They need months, not days or weeks. Every animal is different, and in this day and age, where everyone wants easy, Popeye doesn't fit for them.

It's dogs like Popeye that keep me going. The lost and lonely. Those deserving of love have never found it because they're different—mold breakers.

Just like me.

STONEFACE

THIS ISN'T my first time here in lockup, but it is my first time on this unit. As the officers showed me to my new digs for the next little while, my gaze swept over every visible inch, looking for familiar faces, and most importantly, where the guard center and cameras were located.

"Day room use is open for another twenty minutes," the guard informs me before walking away.

I place my raggedy ass prison bedding on the empty mattress and survey the room. The other bed is neatly made, so I know I have a cellmate, but there are no personal possessions besides toiletries and a small book that looks as if it's meant for a child.

Voices and laughter buzz from the day room below, bouncing off the brick walls. I step out of my cell and look down over the balcony and onto the crowd of men below. Orange seems to be the color here for those of us who don't exactly live a law-abiding lifestyle.

Making my way down the stairs, my eyes travel over every single face, but I don't stare too long. I know better than to look one of these motherfuckers in the eye. What I need to be is observant without being obvious.

My plan to get myself locked up wasn't really a plan, so much as done on a whim. I'd needed to do something —anything—to get myself into Travis County State Jail because *he* was here. And even more unbelievable than that, he was alive.

Both of those facts needed to change—are *going* to change—very, very soon.

That is, if I can find the son of a bitch.

The day room is nothing special. A dozen or so octagon tables with attached benches bolted into the cement floor. A television on mute with closed captioning darting along the bottom of the screen, hanging inside a metal cage in the corner of the room, with six telephones placed in the opposite corner. And front and center is the rounded counter for the guards to observe us all.

The volume in the room has gone down significantly since I walked in, the inmates' eyes following me as I make my way toward an empty table where I can sit with my back facing the wall. No way in hell is anyone taking me by surprise. I may be the focus of everyone's attention, but none of them are of any concern to me, because none of them are Chad Elscher.

The man who ignites a steady burn in my gut. A fire that never stops raging, and never goes away.

He's the man I'm going to kill.

Keeping my eyes toward the silent television, I lose myself in the memory of the newscast I'd seen him on eighteen years ago, of his smug face and emotionless, dead eyes. I haven't seen him since then, but I'll never forget that face, or what he did to get on the news in the first place.

An orange jumpsuit goes soaring by me and crashes into the wall. My eyes snap into focus as six men close in, their faces twisted and cruel as they look past me.

"Get up, mush mouth," one of them jeers. "Get up and fight."

Frowning, I stand and move aside, trying to get a better handle on the situation. The six men move together in a V formation, with the one who had spoken leading the pack.

The man who had hit the wall is a mountain of a man. He's easily six and a half feet tall, and can't be much older than nineteen years old. His muscles, though not defined, are most definitely pronounced, as is his lower lip. He cowers on the floor, his dark-skinned arm wrapped around himself as he stares up at the mob hovering in front of him.

"N-n-n-no," he stutters out. "I w-w-w—"

"W-w-w-w," the man mocks, elbowing the inmate to his right, chuckling. "Learn to fucking talk, dickweed. Now give it to him."

When I finally see the candy bar clutched tightly in the large man's hand, things fall into place.

The man on the floor glances down at his chocolate bar, his lip quivering as he finally holds it out.

They all laugh before the leader of the group steps forward to take the candy from his hand. That's when I decide I can't take anymore.

Stepping forward, I place myself between the two and pin the aggressor with a menacing stare. The name on his uniform says *Howell*, and from the looks of things, *Howell* doesn't like me getting involved.

Too damn bad for Howell.

The man is barely six feet tall. I know this because I'm nearly seven feet tall. This asshole would get lost in my shadow.

"If you're wanting candy, I think it's time you put your own order in for commissary."

"Fuck you, man," he snarls, taking a step closer. "You might be new here, but you'll learn damn fast that I rule this fucking unit, and I will take you down."

Cocking my brow, I tilt my head to the side. "All by yourself? Or do you need your goons here to help you?"

His fist flies out, but I know guys like him. They're

hotheads. They're led by emotion instead of common sense. That means they make mistakes, and Howell has made a big one, because he doesn't know that I'm an expert in mixed martial arts. Though he figures it out pretty quick when I grab his wrist mid-swing and use his own momentum to bring him closer, spin him around, and place him on his knees in front of me with his hand up between his shoulder blades.

I ignore his cries of pain as I glare at the others. They look uncertain, debating on if they should be helping or running for their lives. I hold up my free hand and smirk. "Anyone else?"

The men immediately scatter.

Turning, I drag Howell along and face the man on the floor. "What's your name?"

"B-B-B-Buddy," he replies, sitting up a little straighter, his eyes now void of fear.

I nod. "Nice to meet ya, Buddy. You can call me StoneFace, and this here is..." I give Howell a shake, causing him to cry out again. "This is Howell. Now, I know you know Howell already, but what you don't know is that Howell here is gonna be a whole new man. Aren't you, Howell?"

"Fuck you," Howell spits.

I yank his wrist farther up his back. If I pull up much more, his shoulder will pop right out of its socket. That would suck for him, but I have to admit, I've done it before, and the noise it makes when it pops is fucking cool.

"Aren't you, Howell?" I ask again. "You're gonna stop being a stupid asshole, aren't you? And you're going to stop harassing Buddy and the rest of the men on this unit. Right?"

I tug a little on his wrist.

"Right!" Howell screams.

I see a guard approaching from the corner of my eye, so I speed this up a bit. "Apologize to Buddy."

"I'm sorry," he snarls.

"Did that sound like he's sorry to you?" I ask Buddy.

Buddy's eyes are wide as he watches the scene unfold, but he doesn't speak. Instead, he shakes his head.

"Me neither. Why don't you try that again, Howell?"

The guard has stopped moving. He's not intervening.

"I'm sorry," Howell cries. "I'm sorry, okay? I won't go near you again!"

I look back at Buddy. "Does that work for you?"

He nods, his eyes still wide.

Pulling Howell closer to me, I whisper into his ear, "You, or any of your pals go near Buddy again, I will make sure the only thing left of you for the guards to find will be your nasty ass teeth. *Comprende?*"

Howell gulps, but nods.

Shoving him away, I watch him scurry off in shame

through the crowd of snickering men and up the stairs to his cell, which is the one right next to mine. *Awesome.*

Turning, I extend a hand out to Buddy. "You good, man?"

Buddy takes it and says as I help him to his feet, "You made Howell mad."

"Howell's a pussy," I retort. "He bugs you again, you let me know."

Buddy grins. "Thank you."

I turn then and scan the room. All eyes are on me, including the two guards who had watched the whole thing go down and not bothered to step in. "That goes for every fucking one of you," I call out. "Buddy is off-limits. You fuck with him, I fuck with you."

Nobody says a word, but I know I just made myself a few enemies. I also drew the attention to myself I was hoping to avoid, all within five minutes of being here. That has to be some kind of record.

I glance at the guards again, and the one closest to me nods and walks away. If I didn't know any better, I'd say he'd just given me a stamp of approval. *Interesting.*

DELILAH

"HERE WE GO AGAIN," I mutter as I pull into the tiny parking lot outside of the Travis County State Jail. Finding a spot near the front, I park my van and slump back into the seat. My heart hums inside my chest with the twisting nerves churning in my belly. You'd think after working at the state prison all these years, a county jail wouldn't bother me too much. But the last time I was here, it was under much different circumstances. The program was barely off the ground, and I made so many mistakes in setting it up. Mistakes that nearly cost me my life. Mistakes that I would never forget or allow to occur again now that I'm back. That's why I have my rules.

Rule one of working with inmates? Anything can be used against you. If they want it, they'll make it, take it, or smuggle it in. Protecting myself is, above all else, priority number one. While the prison is more likely to have a riot or rampant violence, the jail is still a dangerous place, even with a lower level of security.

Pulling the visor down in the van, I double check my reflection. My long, dark hair is pulled tightly around the crown of my head in a bun. My gaze then falls down to my outfit. I straighten out my Austin Animal Rescue T-shirt and tuck the hem tightly back into the waistband of my jeans. Feeling around the console, I find my ID from the rescue and clip it to my jeans pocket.

Satisfied, I grab the file with Ashley's notes and step out of the van into the hot Texas heat. It beats down from above against the blacktop, and it doesn't take long before a bead of sweat drips down my brow. It takes a special person to like the Texas heat, and days like today make me question if warm, snow free winters are worth living here.

A few visitors loiter around the front entrance when I approach. None of them look happy to be here—not a single one. Visiting hours are normally in the mornings, so if I had to make a guess, these folks are either here for new inmates or picking them up. With a polite nod and a smile, I slide past the older woman leaning next to the buzzer for the front doors and press the button. A loud voice immediately booms out from the speaker box.

"Name?"

"Delilah Walker, Austin Animal Rescue. I'm here to

meet, um..." I fumble with my file and find the name of the guard. "Jessica Roscoe?"

"One minute," the man huffs out. A few minutes tick by, and a lot more sweat drips from my forehead before a loud buzzing comes from the door to my left. "Walker, report to the front desk."

"Thank you!" I call out, grabbing the door handle. The light shines off the dark cement floor as I make my way to a male guard sitting behind a desk.

At my approach, he looks up and asks, "You the new dog lady?"

"Yes. Owner, actually."

"What happened to the other one?"

"She moved out of town."

He frowns. "Shame. She always brought us cookies. You bake?"

"No, sir, I don't." I laugh. "I'm not much of a cook, let alone a baker. I wouldn't subject y'all to that kind of thing." Truth be told, I mostly ate takeout vegan meals from a local Mom-and-Pop shop down the street. Years back, their son was looking for a volunteer job for his college applications, and I helped him out, so they always give me a discount. With the hours I keep, it just makes things easier. I can't remember the last time I actually made something that didn't come pre-made or out of a can.

"Too bad," he chuckles. "Roscoe will be with you in a

few minutes. She's finishing up her rounds in the women's unit." He points to the left of the main area. "Feel free to head on over to our break room if you'd like to wait there. Might be some donuts left over from the carry-in this morning if you're hungry."

"Thanks." Pivoting, I head off toward the room and push through the cracked door. Thankfully, no one's inside. The man at the front desk was right about the donuts, but I opt for a cup of coffee instead. Being vegan definitely makes finding things on the go harder, but it is what it is. Coffee in hand, I plop down at a smaller table near the back end of the room.

While I wait, I pull out Ashley's notes and review them again. There are thirteen participants currently enrolled in the program, down from fifteen, which is normally our max. The inmates are mostly older men incarcerated for theft or drug-related charges. The youngest man was newly accepted into the program, and had developmental disabilities. Ashley had made special notes in his file about needing to find him the right fit for his new canine companion. She left me a list of a few possibilities, but it normally works best to see which animal connects with the person first. Once I met him, I'd have a better idea of which of our available dogs I should bring with me next time for a trial run.

"Miss Walker?"

I nearly jump out of my skin when I hear my

name being called. My coffee tips over onto my papers and soaks them. Springing into action, I grab a stack of paper towels from the counter next to me and furiously attempt to clean up my mess. *Get it together, Delilah.* Rule number two? Know your surroundings.

"I'm so sorry. I didn't mean to scare you." She stifles a laugh at my expense. "I hope I didn't ruin anything important."

"No, no, this is my fault. I should've been paying more attention." Finally, wiping away the last of my coffee from the table, I toss the soaked paper towels into the trash can, rub my palms on my jeans to dry them off, and extend my hand out to her. "I'm Delilah."

She reaches out and shakes it. "Please, call me Jessica." She's more petite than I expected. Not that I'm tall by any means, but for her line of work, I would've expected someone... well, bigger. "Ready to see the kennels? I have about twenty minutes before I need to relieve someone for their break, so I hope you don't mind walking and talking."

"Not a problem at all. Makes things easier for me, to be honest."

"This way, then." She ushers me out of the break room and down a hallway.

"How long has it been since you've been here?"

"Years. Once we got the program off to a good start,

Ashley took over so that I could establish the program at the state prison."

"Ah. So before the expansion."

"Yes. When we first started the program here, the jail had been much smaller than it is now."

"It'll take some getting used to, but I'll be here to help navigate until you get your GPS set for the layout." We stop at a large intersection of the hallway, and she zips left. As fast as she walks, it's hard to get a feel for the direction we're going.

"Are there other guards that help with the program?"

"Just a few. We've had some personnel shifts over the last few weeks, and we're a bit short-staffed. The new kennel area is heavily monitored, of course, as is most of the building, but I would suggest making sure a guard is with you at all times. Working at the prison, you're probably used to a whole team of them helping out, huh?"

"I wouldn't say a 'team,' but they have dedicated personnel to support the program."

"Wish I could say the same for here, but prisons have bigger budgets than we do. You know how that goes." Unfortunately, I do. AAR lived on donations for care of the animals and our expenses, whereas jails had to rely on tax money from local residents. At least their funds were guaranteed, where ours wavered from month-to-month. Some are better than others.

We twist and turn down a few more hallways before

hitting a dead-end with a large monitored door. Swiping her badge, she ushers me into a large open room that erupts with barking dogs the second we step inside, and gains us everyone's attention.

"Listen up, guys. This here is Miss Walker." She waves her hand in my direction. With a smile, I give a small wave to the audience in the room. "She's taking over for Miss Ashley. You'll treat her with respect, you hear me?"

"Yes, ma'am," a few of them mutter back. One of the older men gives me a smile and wink as we move closer to the kennels, filled with happy, wagging tails. They look spirited and healthy, thriving in a more settled environment, instead of being cooped up inside the rescue in cages. Seeing the success of our hard work with this program fills me with pride.

A bulldog presses his snout into my leg as I pass by the first kennel. He takes in a big whiff and yips. Leaning down, I scratch his ears. "Hey, Diesel. How are you doing, buddy?" He licks my hand and wags his tail like a propeller.

"What have I told you about licking, D? Don't lick the ladies," an older inmate chastises as he approaches me from inside the kennel. "Sorry. We've been working on that."

"This is Ted," Jessica advises. He's the main caretaker for kennel time. Waving for me to move on to the other kennels, she introduces me to everyone, one by one. The last is a giant of a man, sitting on the ground at the back of the kennel room, staring into an empty cage.

"Who's that?"

"Buddy. He's the newest member of the group. Did Ashley mention him?" she whispers.

Something inside my head clicks. He's the participant waiting for his dog. I can see what she meant now by a special dog for a special case.

"Did she bring me my puppy?" Buddy asks with enormous brown eyes that glaze over with sadness when he sees I've come empty-handed.

"I'm sorry, Buddy, I didn't. But when I come next time, I'll bring a new friend for you to play with. That sound okay?"

His face fills with childlike glee. "Do you think the puppy will like me?"

"I think it will. Have you had a puppy before, Buddy?"

"No. My dad wouldn't let me have one." He grimaces. "He didn't want no damn dog in his house." His voice turns cold, and I look at Jessica, who just shakes her head.

"Well, I'm sorry to hear that, but you know what? I'll make sure to bring you the most special dog we have. How does that sound?'

"Can you bring him tomorrow?"

"Maybe not tomorrow, but I'll be back in a few days."

"Tomorrow would be better, but okay." Buddy shifts his gaze back to the empty cage, like if he stares long enough, his dog will magically appear.

Jessica gestures for me to follow her out of the kennel.

"Buddy's certainly interesting," I note.

"He's awaiting trial for murdering his father."

A gasp. "You've got to be kidding, right?"

"Not in the slightest. By all accounts, he's the deadliest man in the program, and you'd do best to keep your eye on him."

"If he's that dangerous, why did he get approved for the program at all? We only allow non-violent offenders to work with the dogs." Better yet, why didn't Ashley run this by me? The criteria we put in place was to protect the dogs from harm. If this man is violent, he shouldn't be around the animals at all.

"The sheriff thought a companion animal would help keep him calm. It's your call now as the program director, but I hope you consider keeping him on. He has yet to show any aggression, so we believe he should be fine working with you, just as he was with Ashley when she was evaluating him with one of the other dogs."

"I'll have to review his file more before I can agree on anything." An instant pang of guilt punches me in the stomach, knowing I made a promise to bring him a dog at my next visit. *Lord have mercy, he may have killed a guy, and I'm worried about hurting his feelings. Come on, now, Walker.*

"While you're doing that, I pulled the files for all the current participants. They're in my office, if you'd like to follow me." Oh, fun. Homework on my first day.

With a silent sigh, I fall in line behind her, and with each step, I wonder exactly how many more surprises Ashley left behind for me.

STONEFACE

A GUARD I hadn't seen before steps inside my cell. "You have a visitor downstairs. I'm heading that way, so I'll take you."

"Not interested," I say, going back to my push-ups.

The guard watches as I pound out another ten and keep going. "Someone's here to see you," he repeats. "Someone cares enough to drive all the way here for you."

Sighing, I get to my feet. "And I'm still not fucking interested."

Instead of arguing, he shakes his head and disappears around the corner.

I don't know exactly who's here to visit me, but I can certainly guess. The Black Hoods MC are the only friends and family I have. They're the only ones who would care I was locked up at all.

They also have no idea about what's going on. They don't know what I'm planning, and they don't need the blowback of my shit stinking up the club for the rest of them. Though whoever's here won't like it, they might as well fuck right off. As soon as I got locked in here, I was no longer a Black Hood.

"StoneFace, guess what!"

I turn to see Buddy striding into my cell, the grin on his face wide enough to block out the sun. "Hey, man. You look happy."

"I am." Plunking his ass down on my bed, his smile grows even wider. "I met Miss Lilah today, and she sure is pretty. She's gonna bring me a puppy next time she comes, and I got a kennel for him already. I got to clean it out, and everybody—"

"Whoa," I say, putting my hand up to stop him. "You're going too fast, pal. What are you talking about? A Lilah, a puppy, and a kennel. What's all that shit?"

Buddy's eyes dance with more excitement than I've ever seen on a grown ass man before. "Miss Lilah is the dog lady. She brings dogs in that have no homes so people like me, who have been bad, still have a chance to have a puppy to love us."

There's a lot to unpack in those few sentences, and I have to really think about which part I want to address first. I have no idea why Buddy's here in lockup. I've never asked because it's none of my fucking business.

Yet what he'd just said, about being bad, has made me genuinely curious.

But he's so happy, so I decide instead to address the other topic. "You're getting a dog?"

Buddy nods so fast, I'm surprised his eyeballs aren't spinning around in their sockets. "A nice one too, and he's gonna love me—I know he will."

I clap my hand down on his shoulder. "That's badass news, bro. Congrats. And, of course, he'll fucking love ya, because dogs are awesome."

He squirms with excitement. "You should see some of the dogs the other guys get to have. Ted has Diesel, and Glover has Rover. Shanks has Boots, and the new guy, Elscher, got to bring his dog with him. Her name is Missy, and she's so pretty, and…"

He's still talking, but I can no longer hear a word he's saying. My ears are ringing, and I suddenly feel like I'm stuck inside a tunnel at just the mention of that motherfucker's name—*Elscher.*

There are nearly two thousand inmates housed here at Travis County Jail. You could be here for five years and still not meet everyone living within these walls. But Elscher is an uncommon name. What are the chances that this *Elscher* fuck that Buddy just mentioned is the one I came here to find?

Buddy's lying back on my bed now, one knee bent, his right ankle crossed over it as he chatters happily about the animal rehab program.

"How do I get in?" I ask, interrupting him again.

"Huh?"

"The dog program. How do I get in?"

Buddy swings his long legs over the side of the bed and sits up. "Oh, it's not just a dog program. There are kitties too. And one guy even has a potbellied pig. I'd love a pig."

Blood rushes through my veins so fast, I can hear every single drop as it makes its journey through my body. "How do I get in?"

Buddy shrugs. "I don't know. One of the guards got me in."

I glance out the door, down to where the guards sit in the bubble, and spot the one who'd given me the nod after sticking up for Buddy. I haven't seen or heard from him since, but the chances of him recommending me would be better if Buddy came along to ask. I could be his protection, help make their jobs a little easier, even.

"You think they'd let me in?"

Buddy looks almost giddy. "Miss Lilah will let you in—she has to!"

I couldn't care less about *Miss Lilah*. I feel a little guilty using Buddy to get me closer to Elscher, but I may not get a chance to otherwise. If I can't get to him, this will all have been for nothing. The last eighteen years will have been for nothing.

"Why don't you come with me and we'll ask?"

"Okay."

Buddy and I make our way down the stairs, heading straight for the bubble, when a man I've never seen before bumps me with his shoulder. Placing something discreetly in my hand, he says in a low voice, "Judge sends his regards."

I turn to see who the man is, but he disappears into a crowd of inmates standing around in a circle, rapping.

I guess that answers the question of who my visitor had been. Judge is the president of the Black Hoods MC, and he wouldn't have taken too kindly to me refusing to see him. I do my best to appear like nothing's happening, and tuck it into the waistband of my pants.

It's sharp and long. There's no question that what I have in my pants is a prison-made knife, otherwise known as a *shiv*.

Fucking Judge.

Buddy's already at the guard station, talking animatedly to the guard, gesturing to me as I approach.

I don't know what he says to the guy, but I don't even have to speak. When I pull up beside Buddy, the guard is already nodding his head. "I'll see what I can do."

DELILAH

"Y'ALL ARE DOING GREAT," I call out to the group.

"Even me?" Buddy's childlike voice rings out from the back of the kennel area.

I laugh. "Yes, you too."

After a thorough review of Buddy's file, as well as a talk with the guards, I had decided to honor Ashley's evaluation. While knowing his history and pending charges in a bit more detail, I can't say that I'm not still hesitant. But the second I brought in Rocco, a standard poodle mix we'd taken in from a hoarding case a few months back, it was love at first sight for them both. Buddy dotes on him, and in the few short days I've been monitoring them together, I realized Ashley and the sheriff were right. Buddy needed this program just as much as Rocco had needed Buddy.

Returning to the rest of the room, I happily check in

with each of the program's participants one-on-one. Like these men, the animals are getting a semblance of their freedom back, and a piece of reality seems to always bring out the best in people, man or pet.

I walk toward an inmate whose back is to me, and my heart sinks as he whips around.

"Miss Delilah. What a surprise!"

Oh, no, no, no. Not him. Please, not him. I thought I'd seen the last of him at the prison, now that one of my volunteers, Bobby, had stepped up to take over for me there for the time being. Why is he here?

"Hello, Chad."

His dog, Missy, shoves her way into the room and barrels into my legs.

"We've been working on how she says 'hello.'"

"She's certainly doing better than expected," I reply, trying to hide the unnerving waver in my voice. Missy had been one of my tougher cases. A former bait dog that didn't take to a single family or trainer until Chad started into the program. He'd asked for a tough nut to crack, and he'd gotten more than his money's worth with her.

Chad tugs back on her leash and puts her in a sit / stay position. "I can't thank you enough for allowing me to bring Missy with me while I'm here."

"Uh, I didn't."

He grins. "I know you had a hand in it."

I didn't, really, but his enthusiasm for his preconceived notion that I had any kind of pull at the jail takes me by surprise. Chad had shown an unhealthy interest in me at the prison from day one. Having him here is problematic for more than one reason, but mostly because the security isn't as restrictive as it is in the prison. For every inmate at the prison program, there's a guard. Here, I'm lucky if I can get a couple of guards for the whole crew.

Keeping a wary eye on Chad and his encroaching proximity, I move away from him and toward Buddy, whose eyes are narrowed at Chad.

"You shouldn't say things like that in front of Miss Walker," Buddy lectures him. "Swearing in front of ladies is wrong."

Chad huffs out a quick laugh. "Whatever you say, big guy."

Eager to get away from Chad, I attempt to distract Buddy. "Show me what Rocco has learned today."

Chad's eyes are still on me. I can feel them on me like a physical thing. Like ten million bugs crawling all over my skin.

Buddy may be dangerous, but Chad is a stone-cold murderer who has spent most of his life in prison. The charges I'd read in his prison file would make a serial killer's skin crawl. He's also the reason I have rule number three: Don't trust anyone.

Chad can be sweet as pie when he wants to be, but his conviction speaks for itself. He made me feel uncomfortable, and I'd wanted him out of my program, but they had transferred him out before I had spoken to the sheriff. That he showed up here with Missy was a shock to me.

I watch as Buddy does some basic commands with Rocco, my mind going over what the hell I'm going to do about Chad. And then he's standing right beside me. I whip my head around in time to see his gaze shifting up and down my body. It's enough to make the twinge of my discomfort noticeable.

"It's nice to see you," he purrs.

I press my lips together and frantically search for a guard. I almost sigh out loud when I see one is already heading our way.

"Leave her alone, inmate."

"She and I are old friends," Chad tells him. "You should let us catch up."

"Not happening. Either tend to your animal, or you'll be back in your cell."

Seeing the opportunity in front of me, I excuse myself, putting some much-needed distance between us.

Moving back toward the other kennels, I spy Jessica entering the room with an enormous beast of a man, two guards flanking him on either side. Neither of them match up to what I can only describe as a fifth of what he could weigh. The guy is massive. He looks like one of those pro wrestlers with a full beard, arms covered in tattoos, and a shiny bald head. He could be a bearded stunt double for Dwayne Johnson, and I love that guy. *Screwed, thy name is Delilah Walker.*

Jessica waves me over, but I hesitate when his eyes lock onto me. Where Chad makes my skin crawl, Dwayne Johnson's doppelganger makes my stomach flip-flop like a gymnast on the uneven bars.

Abort. Ignore him.

His eyes remain on me with every step I take. It's like a one-way staring contest I wish he'd lose already.

Please don't be the new member. Buddy and Chad are enough. I don't need another particularly dangerous big guy. Or, as I like to call them, PDBG, in the room. Not one who's looking like he wants to eat me alive.

I think I'd let him, too.

That thought shocks me. *Down, girl.*

I keep my distance when I finally slow my approach.

"Who's this?"

"Mr.—"

"Call me StoneFace," he replies, cutting Jessica off.

"What kind of name is that?" I blurt out before I can stop myself. My cheeks blush with hot embarrassment.

"The only one I have," he growls, his large, expansive chests jutting out.

"Okay… *StoneFace,*" I gulp. "Whatever makes your freak flag fly."

"This here's your new applicant," Jessica chimes in as she pulls a folder out from under her arm and thrusts it into my hands. *Great. Just freaking great.* This is going to be a problem. Another one that I really, really don't need in the same room right now.

"Oh," I mutter quietly. *Get it together, woman. Do your job.* "Can you tell me about why you're interested in the program?"

"Something to do." Short and sweet answers seem to be his thing. Apparently, staring is also his thing, because he's still doing it.

"Well, okay. Direct and to the point. Do you have any experience with dogs?"

"Yes." Christ on a cracker. Getting anything out of this guy is like trying to pull teeth from a toothless man.

"Care to tell me what kind?" I probe.

"Had them all my life."

"Was that so hard?" I tease.

His cold, hard stare implies that indeed it was.

"When can I start?" he questions, inching closer to me as he talks. Jessica looks at the two guards, who step in front of him, pushing him back. It's not even me he's looking at. He's staring intently at something behind me, his eyes filled with a brewing hostility that both terrifies and excites me.

"The dogs here are already matched with other members. You'll have to wait until my next visit."

"How long?" He tries to move farther into the kennel area, but the guards are quick to react.

"Move back, inmate!" one of them yells.

StoneFace looks down at him like a giant sizing up which ant he's going to step on first. Jessica sidles in closer, talking to him under her breath. I can't hear what she's saying, but his eyes stay on that something behind me. I doubt he's even hearing a single word she's saying to him.

"StoneFace?" I breathe. "I'll bring your dog in a few days, okay?"

He doesn't acknowledge me for a few moments, but then, as if breaking himself out of a spell, he nods. His eyes look away from whatever he'd been staring at, and his body relaxes. His gaze softens as it lands on me.

"Let's go," one of his guards says, pulling him back toward the door. StoneFace doesn't struggle, but he doesn't move easily, either. The door opens, and the trio disappears, the click of the lock snapping me out of my trance.

"You need more than two guards on that guy," I joke.

"Nah. The bigger they are, the quicker they fall in line," she replies. I don't think she even breathes before pulling a one-eighty in the conversation. "So how are things going?"

"Fine, considering this is only my second day back with the program."

"Buddy behaving himself? Seems to like his new friend."

"He's doing well so far today. I think it would be best, though, that instead of having Rocco in his cell with him, we gently introduce him to full-time care of him. I'd like for him to stay in the kennels at night until I deem him ready for a trial run of overnight stays."

"Understood. I'll relay that information to the night shift. They help with the nighttime potty break routines."

"I want to make you aware of an issue that seems to have followed me from the prison. Chad Elscher. He's going to be an issue. Is there any way I can request additional guards?"

"Take it up with the sheriff. That's his call."

"I don't think you understand—"

"I understand perfectly. But pulling guards off the wards to watch this guy falls under the jurisdiction of the sheriff. I'll tell him of your concerns, and put the word out through the other guards, but I can't snap my fingers and *poof* guards into the room."

"What exactly do you suggest I do?"

"Keep your distance from him the best you can until we can sort something out."

Easier said than done, since I'm locked in the room

with him. While Buddy is big, Chad might scare me a little more.

I nod my head in agreement, but I'm feeling anything but agreeable. Until the sheriff makes the call, I'm on my own with a convicted killer, a possible murderer, and a bearded Dwayne Johnson, all in the same room. What could possibly go wrong?

STONEFACE

LAYING eyes on Elscher for the first time was like being dunked in a pool of ice water. Every bit of rage and disdain, and pure, unbridled hatred I have for that man came bubbling to the surface and nearly boiled over.

It may well have to. If that brunette chick with the nice rack hadn't been there, it likely would have.

I don't know what it was about her. Her soft voice? Her southern twang, perhaps? Whatever it was, I'd been working out a plan on how to break away from those guards, and Elscher right there in front of everyone. It was her saying my name that broke my train of thought.

I could've done it too. Those guards were fucking nothing compared to eighteen years of pent-up rage. And the other inmates? They would've been fine as long as they stayed out of it. Otherwise, I'd have ended those motherfuckers too.

"Rocco sure does like those bacon treats," Buddy says, grinning to himself as he fills out his commissary order form. "He practically ate the whole bag. Miss Lilah told me next time to only give him bits at a time, but that doesn't seem fair, does it? He's a big dog. He needs big treats."

I grunt and look down at my form. Fucking commissary. I could not care less about the mundane tasks of this damn jail. Who needs chips, deodorant, and ramen fucking noodles anyway?

People in here act like getting commissary is Christmas goddamn morning.

A large hand clamps down on my shoulder. "Visitor. And I suggest you don't blow this one off. Judge wouldn't like that."

I look up at the guard's face, and am surprised to see that I recognize him. I don't remember his name, but I've seen him around the clubhouse a few times. A friend of the club, and apparently, a guard at Travis County Jail.

I look back down at my commissary form. "Not interested."

My ass is out of the seat before I can say another word, and I'm suddenly standing nose to nose with the guy. He's just as big as I am, and he looks pissed.

"Listen, man. Judge is done fucking around with you. He said to let you know that you owe them an explanation, and if you don't go, there will be hell to pay."

Fuck.

I'm not afraid of Judge necessarily. I'm not really afraid of anything at all. But I have a mission, and if Judge gets his balls in a twist over me ignoring the club, he might make it difficult for me to complete it.

Sighing, I nod once and tell Buddy I'll be back.

The guard leads me out of the unit and down a long cement hallway to an elevator. Once inside, he pushes the button for the third floor, and we begin our descent.

"How do you know Judge?"

"Not your business," is all he says. *Ballsy motherfucker.*

The door opens, and he leads me to a room where there are booths with stools, a telephone, and a glass window showing an identical booth on the other side.

And there at the third booth sits GreenPeace, one of the Black Hoods, with a smirk on his face the size of Texas. "Surprise!"

I don't hear the word, but I know exactly what he's saying by the way his lips move. In his shoes, I'd make a shitty joke too, but he's on that side of the glass, and I'm in here.

I sit, my arms folded, and glare at a spot high above his head. I see him motioning for me to pick up the phone receiver in my peripheral vision and feel instantly torn.

GP has been my brother for years. We have had each

other's backs. He doesn't deserve this. None of the Hoods do.

Groaning, I snatch the receiver off its cradle and press it to my ear. "Go home, GP."

GP's brows lift in surprise. "Not even a 'Hi, GP? I've missed you, GP'? Pretty harsh, don't you think?"

"Go. Home."

GP stares at me then, his posture going rigid, his eyes flashing with anger. "You know what? Fuck you, man. That's not how this works, and you fucking know it. You're a member of a club, asshole. A brotherhood. And you went and did something stupid as fuck—hilarious, mind you, but still, it was stupid as fuck—and then you go fucking radio silent? That's not gonna fly. Not gonna fly with me, and sure as hell not with Judge."

I hold his glare. He's right, that much I know, but he doesn't know the whole story. He doesn't know why I did what I had to do.

"Tell Judge I'm out. Take my patch. I don't want it anymore."

GP gapes at me. "You don't want it? You don't fucking want it? What the fuck, man? You don't get to make that kind of decision. That's not how it works."

I lean forward. "I had a life before the Black Hoods, GP. A really fucked-up life. There was some unfinished business from back then, and now it's time to finish it once and for all."

GP throws a hand up in the air. "Let the club help you, asshole. That's what we do."

An ache rips at my heart, but I ignore it, burying the emotion down deep. "This doesn't touch the club. I'll deal with my shit, alone."

"What shit, man?" GP's face is red, and I can see one of the little veins at his temple throbbing as he squeezes the phone receiver tighter in his hand. "What shit are you dealing with?"

"See ya, GP."

Placing the phone in the cradle, I turn to walk away, while GP's muffled voice screams from the other side, "What shit? StoneFace! What shit?"

I don't look back.

Walking away from the club is the only way I can do this. I need to keep them clean. I need to end this once and for all, even if it means walking away from them.

DELILAH

"JUST LOOK AT THE DAMN FILE," I berate myself.

The file in question is the one on the new inmate Jessica brought in under heavy guard to see me last week, and has been sitting on my desk, taunting me all weekend. I pace the floor, muttering, "It's just a file, for crying out loud, not his diary. Read the thing." Back and forth I go, wearing a hole in the already worn linoleum of my office floor before I sigh in frustration.

What is it about this guy that has me so on edge? *He's an inmate. He's on the inside, you're on the outside. It's not going to happen.* Besides, the guy is a complete asshole. It didn't take more than a few sentences strung together by him to figure that out. That's the last thing I need in my life right now. *Jesus. Why did that even pop into my head?*

Bristling up my courage, I plop down into my seat

and throw open the manilla envelope, only to have his black-and-white photo staring back at me. I lean in and study it closely. A wide jawline and cheekbones poke out from under his bristly, long beard, but it's his dark eyes that grab my attention. Even on paper, I can feel the intensity of his dark eyes on me, just like in person. How is that even possible? A quiver runs down my spine, feeling as if he's in the room with me now.

Nope. Not today, doppelganger. Grabbing a Post-It note from my desk, I stick it over his photo. *Now you see me, now you don't.* I shift my focus down to actual words in his file and away from his photo.

Rhett Darby. So, he does have a name. I mean, of course he does, but seeing it makes it more real. Why does he go by such an odd nickname, then? It's not like his name is awful. Hell, it could be much worse. Just ask my cousin Hubert. My aunt and uncle loved older names from the family. Thank God my parents didn't. With my luck, they would have named me after my great-aunts Hortense or Leafa.

The rest of his file isn't what I would've expected. Driving under the influence, grand theft auto of a law enforcement vehicle, and a slow speed case. I frown. How do you have a slow speed chase? I burst out in laughter at the thought of that big man in a cop car driving like grandma on a Sunday. He either has a wicked sense of humor, or has a screw loose.

A knock on my office door interrupts my laugh. "Come in."

Bridgette, one of our local college weekend volunteers, pops her head inside. "Someone's having a good day," she remarks. "I haven't seen you smile that like since I started working here."

"What's up, buttercup?" I greet her, ignoring that little comment.

"There's an older man here who wants to talk to you."

"Oh? Why's that?"

Her face goes slack. "He's here to surrender his dog."

"Oh."

Another one. That makes four just this week. Normally, surrenders trickle in here and there, but this many in one week, not related to a hoarding case or puppy mill, is very odd. Pushing away from my desk, I stalk over to the door and follow Bridgette into the lobby. A frail-looking man sits on a bench with a beautiful Yorkshire Terrier sitting on his lap. He strokes her lovingly, speaking softly to her as we approach.

"Hi, I'm Delilah."

He gently lifts the dog from his lap and tries to stand when I extend out my hand.

"Please, sit. I'll come to you." Smiling, I take a seat next to him on the bench.

"I'm Howard," he begins, his voice shaky and weak. "And this is Penelope."

Penelope looks cautiously at her owner before he nods, and she shifts her head to give my hand a sniff before licking it.

"It's nice to meet you both. Bridgette tells me you're here to surrender your dog. Can I ask why?"

He continues to stroke her fur as he speaks. "My wife, Dolores, passed away a few months back."

"I'm so sorry to hear that, Howard. My condolences."

"Thank you." He takes a deep breath. "I've taken care of my dear Dolores for the last several years after she got sick with cancer. After she died, my health started declining, and taking care of Penelope has been much harder on me. We can't go for our long walks anymore. She loves those, you see." His frail hand shakes as a few tears fall from his weathered eyes. Penelope leans hard into his hand, trying to comfort him.

"She obviously loves you."

"She's been my best girl since Dolores passed on. We do… well, we *did*, everything together."

My heart cracks at that statement. The longer he talks, another piece of my heart chips away with his tears.

"Penelope is certainly lucky to be loved so much by you, Howard, but are you sure this is what you want to do?"

"I'm having surgery tomorrow, and the doctors tell me there's a chance I won't walk out of there. He presses the tips of his fingers to his chest. "Bad ticker."

"Oh, no," I gasp. How scared he must be with that knowledge. I know I'd be terrified if our roles were reversed.

"I can't go into that hospital knowing Penelope would be left alone, so I came here. She's all I have left."

"You don't have to surrender her, Howard. We have other options. Fostering, for example. One of our amazing volunteer families could foster Penelope until you get back on your feet. We do that for a lot of people who live on their own."

"As nice as that idea is, Miss Delilah, Penelope deserves to be with someone who can keep up with her and go on those long walks. If I make it through the surgery, I'll be moving into an assisted living facility permanently. I can't take her with me, as much as I'd like to do that."

The last chunk of my heart breaks away in my chest. He really doesn't have any options other than surrendering her to our care. As much as I hate that he's forced to make this kind of decision, his situation deems it necessary.

"I understand," is all I can muster up to say.

He reaches down next to his leg and pulls a bag onto his lap. "I put all of her favorite toys and treats in this bag. Her bed and stuffie, BunBun Baby, are in there as well." He passes it over to me. "I put the last of her food in there, the stuff she really likes. I wrote the name down on a piece of paper and where I buy it."

"That's so helpful. Thank you."

"Promise me something. Make sure whoever takes her home will love her as much as I do. She's a special girl."

"She'll go home with the best family, Howard, I promise you that. If you'd like, I can see if the adopters would be open to letting her see you, if you'd be interested in that?

He sighs, but smiles. "I'd like that. Just to know she's happy would be enough for me."

"If you can leave me the information of which facility you're going to be staying in after your surgery, I'll be sure to pass it along." Bridgette walks over to the front desk and grabs a pen and pad of paper. Handing it to him, he scribbles down the information and hands it back to her.

"You're a good woman, ma'am. Not many people would have sat here listening to an old man drivel on about his woes like this."

Reaching out, I take his hand in mine and give it a squeeze. "Sitting here with you and Penelope is why I do this job—helping animals and people." Squeezing mine back, he pulls it away and pets on Penelope.

"Do you mind if I sit here a little longer with her?"

"You can sit here as long as you like. Take as much time as you need."

Giving them both some space, I take Bridgette with me back behind the front counter. We both watch from afar with tears in our eyes as Howard and Penelope say their goodbyes. He whispers loving words to her, petting and hugging her for over an hour. Then, with tears in his eyes, he places her in my arms and waves one last goodbye before disappearing out the door. Penelope whimpers in my arms, watching him.

"Shh, shh, Penelope. It'll be okay," I try to reassure her with calm tones as I feel her heart breaking in my arms.

STONEFACE

"NO," I say, sneering at the tiny creature cowering against Delilah's ample tits. "Not only no, but fuck no."

Delilah stands a little taller. "It's not a question, Mr. Darby. This is the dog you're being assigned."

Everyone is watching now. I can feel their eyes on us. "First of all, I told you my name is StoneFace, not Mr. Darby. Mr. Darby was my old man, and my old man was a fucking prick. And second, that ain't a dog. It's like a hairy mole rat or some shit. I'll take a different one—any different one—'cause there's no way I'm taking that."

Delilah's eyes narrow as she takes a step toward me. "StoneFace is not your actual name, and you're in no position to tell me if you're taking this poor creature or any other one in my care. Might I remind you, *sir*, that you are an inmate at this facility, and I have graciously given you a spot in *my* program. This dog was surrendered to me last night by a poor old man who was undergoing heart surgery this morning, and was afraid he wouldn't make it."

Her voice rises as she talks, her face turning a brighter shade of red with each passing second. Her finger comes up and pokes me in the chest. The guard steps forward to object, but I raise my hand to stop him.

"I'll have you know, I got a call from that kind man's friend just a little bit ago, and he didn't make it. He died on that operating table, and now Penelope is scared and alone."

She pokes me again, harder this time.

"And you, StoneFace, may be some big, scary, macho dude, but if you can't show a little compassion to this poor little girl, then you have no place in my program. So what's it gonna be?"

I gape at her. I'm a man of few words on a good day, but I've never been rendered speechless before.

I mull over her words, and after a moment, I reach for the leash dangling from her hand. "I'll take her, but I ain't fucking calling her Penelope. Stupidest fucking name I've ever heard."

Delilah's jaw ticks. "Penelope is the only name this dog knows."

Taking the dog from her, I cock my brow. "And StoneFace is the only name I know. You refuse to call me by that name, and I refuse to call this dog by her sissy fucking name."

The little ball of fur is so light and tiny in my hands. Gently, I turn her until I'm holding her out, putting us eye to eye. "From now on, your name is Penny. Still a sissy name, but better than Penelope."

Delilah's mouth twitches with a hidden smile when Penny's tiny tongue flicks out and licks the tip of my nose.

What the fuck have I gotten myself into?

"Fine." Smirking, she takes a step back. "Penny it is." She points to an area of the kennel with open greenery and a few benches. "Why don't you take her over there and get to know one another?"

Placing Penny on the ground, I cringe at how tiny she is as I walk along beside her. It'll take a conscious effort on my part not to step on the poor little thing. One misstep, and she'll be flat as a pancake.

Together, we make our way to an empty bench. I choose it for two reasons. One, it allows me to act as if I'm getting to know this furball like Delilah had instructed. Two, it's the perfect angle for me to see every other person in the program.

Including Chad.

I plop the tiny dog onto my lap and pet her head as I watch the man I'm going to kill.

He's oblivious, of course. He has no idea who I am,

but he will. I'd never actually met the man, but my name will be the last one he ever hears, my face the last one he ever sees. My life will be the last one he ever ruins.

"Is that your dog?" Buddy asks, sidling over with Rocco at his side. I don't know which one of them has a bigger smile.

"So she says," I grumble, continuing to watch Chad.

How can someone so evil look so normal? How can he just be here, playing with a dog without a care in the fucking world, while on the inside, I'm being scalded by the intensity of my own rage.

"She's pretty," Buddyhere says, reaching his over-sized hand out to pet Melanie, or Felony, or whatever the fuck her prissy little name is. "And she's little. Perfect fit, I'd say."

I don't respond.

Chad is standing beside his dog, but now he's not doing any training. His eyes are on Delilah, and I don't like the way he's watching her one bit.

Delilah isn't exactly my favorite person at the moment—especially after forcing little Peepee here on me—but I know how Chad operates, and he needs to remove his fucking eyeballs from her general direction before I pluck them out with my bare hands and feed them to little Celery here.

"What's her name?" Buddy asks, petting her thick, fluffy fur.

"Don't remember," I reply, still watching Chad.

"You gotta know her name," Buddy prods. "She's your dog. How can you not even know your dog's name?" His voice goes a little higher with each word, and his obvious distress snaps me out of my daze.

"Hey," I say, placing a hand on his shoulder. "It's no big deal, Buddy. She doesn't even know her own damn name."

"Yes, she does! Dogs know their name."

"Everything okay over here?" Delilah asks as she approaches the bench, her eyes cautious as she watches Buddy.

"No," Buddy tells her. "He doesn't even know her name. He needs to remember it, or she'll be sad."

Glaring at me, she plucks the tiny dog off my lap. "Her name is Penelope," she reminds me, cuddling her close, whispering soothing words I can't quite hear from her perfectly shaped lips.

"Penny," I declare, finally remembering our conversation. Fucking Elscher being around is doing nothing for my concentration. "I'll be calling her Penny."

Penny's ears perk up at her new-*ish* name. Hell, she looks like she's smiling at me.

Buddy's megawatt smile is back. "I think she likes it."

"I think you'd be wise to remember it," Delilah warns, handing the dog back over and walking away.

I watch her ass move as she walks, her jeans tight over ample curves.

I think you'd be wise to watch how you speak to me, Miss Delilah. I could definitely handle the opportunity to spank that perfect ass of yours.

DELILAH

"HERE WE GO AGAIN," I mutter after being let into the kennels by a new guard. I'm not in here two seconds before Chad and Missy make a beeline for me. *Great*. Just like at the prison. I couldn't shake this guy, no matter how hard I tried, and that was in maximum security. At least there, I had more eyes to watch and protect me from his advances. Not exactly the case here at the jail.

Missy slams into my legs, causing me to stumble back.

"Funny we keep running into each other." Chad smiles. "Missy and I have been missing you."

I cringe at his smile. There's nothing funny about it. *The only reason it keeps happening is because I haven't figured out a way to get you out of my program, creep.*

The sheriff has been dodging my calls for days, and his secretary keeps giving me excuse after excuse about why he isn't available. One way or another, I'll be talking with him and getting Chad booted the first chance I get. He has to go, or I may have to suspend the program until I can find someone else to do it. I really don't want to take that away from the people who really need it, like Buddy.

"I'm sorry, but I need to check in on Buddy."

"Buddy doesn't need your attention. He's fine. Big guy is out walking his dog anyhow." Shit, he's right. He's not in the room.

"I'll just go check on the other guys. If you'll excuse me." I try to sidestep him, but he mimics me. "Chad, you need to let me do my job." I peer over at the guard behind me, whose attention is on his phone. Shit. No help coming from him unless I make a scene—a really big one.

"We've barely had a chance to talk since I came here."

That would be on purpose, but yet again, here I am, trying to dodge you like Typhoid Mary.

"It's a big class, Chad. I have to check in with everyone." *Lie better, Delilah. Think of something better than that.*

"No, you're not," he argues. "Talk to me. I came here to see you."

The cold, hard truth is that he's here only because he has a court date coming up. Of all the places he could wind up, it had to be another facility where my rescue has a program. It couldn't be a supermax on the east coast, or the damn North Pole. Nope, it's the jail in my town. *Lucky* me.

"Chad, seriously. If you don't back off a bit and let me work, I'm going to call that guard over."

He cranes his neck to look over his shoulder. "Doesn't look like he cares that I'm here." He turns back to face me. "It hurts to know you'd do that to me. I thought we were friends."

"We aren't friends. You're an inmate, and I'm a volunteer."

"I'd like to be friends. Maybe even something more."

It takes everything I have not to vomit the contents of my stomach onto the floor in front of him. *Friends?* The guy is off his rocker, more so than I previously thought if he thinks we have even a platonic relationship.

"Absolutely not." I draw my hand up between us, palm out.

"Come on, Delilah…"

"It's Miss Walker to you."

"I'll call you whatever you want me to, honey, as long as I can…" He trails off, staring off behind me.

"I think the lady said no. Move along," Mr. Darby's deep voice growls out from behind me. Chad's brows furrow, and a flush of red anger stains his cheeks. *Shit.* A pissing match between fuck no Chad and the sexy doppelganger. Can this day get any worse?

"You may be a big motherfucker, but the bigger they are, the harder they fall."

Mr. Darby sidles up next to me on the right, and Penelope moves between all of us, growling at Missy.

"Try me. I eat little shit-for-brains guys like you for breakfast, and I'm still fucking hungry afterward.

Chad's nostrils flare. He has to know he has no chance against a big guy like Mr. Darby. Even if he tried his luck, the guard—well, maybe the guard—would have him on his stomach and in cuffs before he ever got a second chance to swing.

"I'll be back," he warns, jerking Missy's leash as he walks back to his kennel space.

Darby laughs. "No, you won't." He then turns his attention to me. "You okay?"

"Fine," I mutter, wrestling with the need to thank him, but decide to drop it. *Stick to the rules.*

Penelope jumps around my ankles, yipping with happiness. I pet her fluff, and she melts into my hand. Mr. Darby clears his throat, and Penelope leans away from my grasp and turns to him, wagging her tail. His face switches back to staring more at me, which seems to be his favorite pastime as of late. I can be on the other side of the room, and I can feel the heat from his stare, following my every move. Like he's hunting his prey.

"Watch this." He gives her a basic list of commands: sit, lay down, paw, stay. She obeys every single one of them with zero hesitation. "Pretty good, right?"

"Good job, Penelope," I cheer, handing her one of the special treats I had brought along with me to test out on her. She sniffs it in my hand before snatching it away.

"What about me?"

"Good job?" I tease. "Want a treat too? I'd give you a pat on the head, but the guards kind of frown on that kind of fraternization."

"Guards don't scare me." He cocks his brow. "I'd need something a little more..."—he looks me up and down with that heated stare of his—"substantial than a pat on the head, though."

"Uh, well..." I stammer out. He steps a little closer, bringing the heat of his large body close enough that I can smell the woodsy scent of his shampoo. Too close. *Way* too close.

Penelope, taking full advantage of the distraction, pushes up on her back legs to take the treat bag out of my hand and scurries behind her new best buddy. He leans down and takes them away from her, giving her a firm, "No," in his deep, commanding tone, causing her to shrink back.

"I guess she likes those."

"It's a treat. All dogs like treats."

"You'd think that, but you couldn't be more wrong.

I was fostering an animal that would only eat broccoli florets as a treat. Granted, he was on an all green bean diet for the first few weeks after he came into the rescue thirty pounds overweight, but he still loved them."

"The fuck?" he chuffs. "Broccoli? Who gives a dog broccoli?"

"Me? Vegetables are great for dogs."

"Dogs need protein. A skinny thing like her could use a steak, maybe five." Penelope looks up at him and licks her lips. He's not wrong. Protein is essential to animal diets. I just don't agree with where it comes from. "Bet you could eat through a big, fat, juicy steak, couldn't ya, Penny?" My stomach rolls at the image of her doing just that.

"Penelope is the perfect size for her breed. Yorkies are meant to be small," I counter, trying to shake it off. "Besides, there are other ways to get protein that don't involve meat or animal by-products. Nuts and lentils for one, even tofu. Not that I would give her that, but there are plenty of plant-based dog foods on the market right now."

"Let me guess, you're one of those anti-meat activists? You know, the ones who throw red paint on people at fashion shows and shit?"

"Not all vegans are members of P.E.T.A."

"Of course you are." He rolls his eyes at me playfully.

Or, at least, I think it was meant to come off that way. "Figures."

"What's that supposed to mean exactly?" I fire back.

"Nothing," he hisses, his body going rigid when he realizes we're not alone. Turning, I find Chad is back again.

"Time for you to go, big guy. She has other people to work with. Isn't that right, Miss Walker?" He almost coos out that last part. A stinging reminder of the words I had used on him.

A waft of red-hot anger tickles against my skin when Mr. Darby moves closer, and Penelope puts herself between Chad and me yet again. Taking one sniff of him, she bites down hard on his ankle. Chad yelps in surprise and pain.

"Good girl," Mr. Darby praises her, smiling.

"A dog like that shouldn't be in a program. She's a menace," Chad huffs.

Darby bristles up again, but the guard finally takes notice and yells out to the group, "Time's up. Leash 'em up and get in line, inmates."

"Run along, now," StoneFace chastises with a dismissive wave of his large hand. Chad's response is a frustrated growl before he stomps off toward Missy's kennel.

"Thanks for that."

"Anytime, Flower Child. See you soon." His deep, teasing voice is like a lover's promise whispered in the wind. A wind that can't be blowing right now. This is a no wind zone.

Snapping a leash to Penelope's collar, the two of them trot off to the line of inmates outside the door, leaving me standing here in a stupor.

Over his shoulder, he yells out, "Rain check on that treat?" and winks as he walks out the door.

STONEFACE

NOT BOTHERING to look up at the guard, I tell him, "I'm not going. I already said my piece to the club."

Without warning, his hand is on my bicep and he's spinning me around, pressing my face to the painted brick wall. I haven't even had a chance to react before the cuffs are on my wrists.

The blood pounds through my veins as I turn and gape at him. "What the fuck, man! I have a right to refuse visitors!"

This guy again. And this time, I'm able to see his name badge—*Johnson*.

Well, if that isn't the most common fucking surname in all of North America, I don't know what is. "Who the fuck are you?" I ask again, my feet moving double-time to keep up as he shoves me down the hall toward the elevator.

Once the door closes, and it's just the two of us, Johnson leans closer to avoid being detected by the camera's microphone. "The Black Hoods have helped my family many times. I owe Judge my life, and you owe him some fucking respect."

I turn and sneer. "Fuck you, man. You don't know one damn thing about me."

"I know this is the third time the club has been by, and only the second time you're seeing them. I know the first time you didn't tell them a fucking thing. Judge is ready to rip this jail down to its foundations, just to rip you a shiny new asshole."

I let out a long, low sigh, and my chin drops to my chest. "They're supposed to let this shit go."

The elevator door opens, and Johnson leads me out the door and into the visitation room. Just as I reach the seat, Johnson remarks, "Family doesn't just let shit go."

My ass hits the seat, and I force myself to look ahead, straight into Judge's angry eyes.

In many ways, Judge is kinda like a father to me. A swearing, motorcycle riding father who isn't afraid to kick my ass if I step out of line. Lord knows, he's been more of a father to me than my own father had been.

My father had walked out on us when I was five years old, leaving my mom to work three jobs just to make ends meet. She literally worked herself into an early grave, dying at just fifty-two years old, two days after I had graduated high school.

I rarely think about that time in my life. Hell, I rarely think about my past at all. But Judge sitting there, glaring at me from the other side of the thick glass, reminds me of just how far I've come. And before I have a chance to shut it down, his angry face also reminds me of exactly what I'm giving up.

Grabbing the receiver from its cradle, I press it to my ear and look at the very pissed off, very large president of the Black Hoods MC.

"Explain," is all he says, his tone leaving zero room for argument.

My chest feels as if a trailer load of Harley's has been parked on top of it, and it's all I can do to keep on breathing, as if everything is okay. "Not much to explain," I say. "I had a life before this club, Judge, and some unfinished business from way back then has popped up. I'm here to finish it."

"What business?"

Yeah, he's pissed. Judge isn't necessarily the chattiest man I know, but these short, gruff responses tell me all I need to know about where I stand in his eyes right now.

I draw in a breath, but my lungs feel as if they're being crushed by the weight of this moment. "No disrespect, Judge, but this is in regard to my family. It has nothing to do with the Black Hoods, and is none of your concern."

Judge's nostrils flare. His face lights with rage for a fraction of a second before he composes himself. "When you were patched into the club, the Black Hoods MC became your fucking family. You are a part of it whether you want it or not. Hell, whether *we* want it or not. Right now, I'd rather kick your ass than try to help you, but that's not how shit goes in a family. You don't just walk away."

"Judge—"

"Shut the fuck up," he growls. "You had your chance to speak, and you spoke wrong. Now it's your turn to listen, and you're going to tune those big fucking ears of yours in and listen close."

Leaning forward, he presses the tip of his finger against the glass, pointing right at me. "Whatever your reasons, you fucked up not coming to me before pulling that stunt with stealing the police car. We'll deal with that, but first, we have some other business to attend to. You remember Henry Tucker?"

That name brings on a whole new wave of anger. How could I forget Henry Tucker? That man had fathered and sold off his own woman as a sex worker and then wanted to do the same with his children.

He'd attempted to kill Judge and his old lady when they took in those kids, and he'd shot Karma and Lindsey, causing her to lose her baby, and Karma to nearly lose his life.

"Yeah," Judge says, his eyes narrowed. "I see you know exactly who I'm talking about. But, did you know he's here in this jail?"

I freeze.

It never sat right with me that Henry Tucker hadn't met his maker at the hands of one of the Black Hoods. The slimy fucker had gotten arrested before we'd had a chance at retribution, and he's been out of touch ever since.

Judge knows better than to say the words, but when our eyes meet, I know what he's telling me. Henry Tucker needs to die.

"Looks like you have a lot of shit to sort out," he says, with more meaning behind his words than anyone listening in would ever understand. "You get your shit handled and we'll talk soon. And the next time I come in here, you better grow a set of balls and come down here like a man without me having to get Johnson to drag you down here by the short and curlies. We clear?"

Memories of Lindsey's tears and Karma struggling to ride his motorcycle after being shot by Henry Tucker play over and over again in my mind.

"I said, are we fucking clear?"

I meet his glare with a new outlook. My own mission

is still very much important, but now I have another one. Now I need to do something for my club.

I nod.

Judge studies me a beat before he says, "You can't run from your family, son. We may be a fucked-up crew, but we've got each other's backs, always. Even when it's not wanted."

Slamming the receiver back into the cradle, he gets to his feet and leaves the room.

Jesus. I should've known I couldn't just walk away, but bringing this shit to my club isn't going to happen either.

I need to get this done. Get Henry Tucker. Get Chad Elscher. And after all that, if the club wants to have my back from the other side of these iron bars, then so be it. But I still have to do what I came here to do.

DELILAH

"SHE LOOKS LIKE A DROWNED RAT." I look down at Penelope in the small basin I had brought with me to groom her. None of the other dogs in the program require the extensive grooming she does, which is why I normally use those dogs in the program. But with Penelope, I had to switch things up a bit. It took a little convincing, but Jessica finally relented in letting me give StoneFace a one-on-one lesson under the watchful eyes of two guards. She's set us up in a rec room instead of in the kennels.

I had to stifle a laugh as I watched him wrestle with her to keep her in the tub. Between jumping in and out, and shaking water all over him, she's having just as much fun as I am watching the show. Who'd have thought such a tiny little creature could frustrate such a big man?

"Stay in the damn tub," he orders when she hops out again. Running around the room in a wide circle, she shakes off the water every step of the way, her feet sliding all over the floor. When she comes close to him, he snatches her up and tosses her back into the soapy water. Her fur is plastered to her tiny little body as she shivers, staring up at him like he's a traitor for keeping this up. He gives her one last rinse before pulling her from the tub and wrapping her body in the fluffy tie-dye towel I'd brought with me.

"Explain to me why the fuck I have to do this?"

"Her breed requires regular grooming. If her hair gets too long, it'll mat. Let that go too long, she'll have to be shaved."

"So she's high-maintenance?" he quips jokingly. "Just like all females."

"Oh, it's not just baths, big guy. She needs to be brushed daily."

"Next thing you're going to tell me is that she needs bows."

Stifling my laughter, I reach into my pocket and pull out two sets. "Hot pink or purple?"

"Ah, hell no," he groans. "I draw the line at bows. Not doing that shit." He tries to puff out his chest, but it only makes me want to poke the bear more.

"Big guy like you afraid of bows? That's a first."

"I'm not afraid of shit," he growls, narrowing his

eyes. Penelope wiggles in his arms, and he lowers her down to the floor between us, setting her free of the towel. Her wet fur, though starting to dry, resembles a bad morning of bed hair.

"Except for bows on a teacup size dog."

"If you haven't noticed, this is a jail, not some high-end fashion mall, Flower Child. I have a reputation to uphold."

He has to be joking, right? Other than Buddy, he's the biggest guy I've seen here. I don't think two little bows on a froufrou dog is going to hurt him in any way. Except for maybe bruising his ego.

"You know, jail makes so much more sense. I just thought you all liked wearing matching outfits and playing with handcuffs like some kinky school girl fetish sex club." His mouth drops before he lets out a hearty laugh. It makes me smile more than it should. "So you do know how to laugh."

He falls silent, but his lips twitch when he says, "Don't get used to it."

"Is that why you want to be called StoneFace?"

StoneFace rolls his eyes at me and crosses his arms over his expansive muscular chest. Large veins pop at his biceps, and I have to divert my eyes from them to keep from staring. The water from Penelope's escapes have soaked his shirt, highlighting every bulging ripple of his chest under his white cotton T-shirt. Whatever he did before being locked up, apparently a healthy gym routine was a part of it, and it's distracting the fuck out of me. *Abort. Look away.* He instantly takes notice. *Shit. Too late.*

"Like what you see, Flower Child?"

"I have no idea what you're talking about," I reply. The room feels like it's gone up several degrees as heat pools between my legs. *Rule four. Rule four. Rule four. Don't fall in love with an inmate.*

He inches closer to me, but the guards clear their throats in a warning. He lowers his voice to a deep whisper. "You look a little flushed."

"I do not."

"Lying's not your strong suit, Flower Child."

"Why do you keep calling me that?"

"Because I can."

"I wish you wouldn't."

"Too bad." Pivoting away from me, he leans down and picks up the water basin. With him, it's like trying to talk to a moody teenager. He's figured out how to press my buttons, and he keeps smashing away at them for sport.

"Wow. All show and no go, big guy."

Shaking his head, he passes by me with the tub full of water, pretending to stumble and splashing it all over me before I can move out of the way. "Oops." Soaking through my T-shirt, it drips down my jeans and into my socks.

He laughs. "My kind of show, Flower Child."

I glare at him, but the guards rush over and push him away from me, barking at him to step back and drop the basin onto the ground.

"You okay, Miss Walker?"

I try to wave them off. "I'm fine, guys. It was an accident."

StoneFace huffs loud enough for all of us to hear. The guard takes a long look at him before turning back to me. "I think we're done here."

"We were just starting to have some fun, fellas."

"Get your animal," the larger guard orders.

StoneFace whistles, and Penelope comes running, stopping next to his feet. "Good girl. You come when you're told." The way he says it sends goose bumps up and down my arms.

He's talking to the dog. Stop making out that every little thing the man says is him flirting, because he's not flirting with me. He's an inmate. End of story. Walk away before you fall too far down the rabbit hole.

"Hang on," I tell the guard before turning to our makeshift wash station. Grabbing her collar, leash, and brush, as well as the bows, I hand them all to him under the watchful eyes of the guards.

"Don't forget to brush her." His hand brushes against mine, and a charge of electricity zings down my spine at his touch. Winking, he pulls away. "And the bows."

"No bows," he declares as the guard shoves him toward the door.

I watch him walk out the door before I allow myself to relax from the runaway train wreck that's coming my way if I don't pump the brakes, and fast. Whatever happened today with StoneFace ends now. I just wish my head agreed with the rest of my body.

STONEFACE

PENNY SITS on my lap like a perfect little doll while I try to jam my giant sausage finger through the impossibly tiny elastic band on one of the bows Delilah had given me.

Snap.

"Oh, for fuck's sake. I quit." Tossing the useless bow across the cell, I place Penny on my mattress and jump to my feet.

My cellmate doesn't move from his position on his bed, but he does tip his book a little so he can see me over the top of it.

"Everything okay?"

Despite having been an inmate here for a couple of months, I haven't really gotten to know Gibbs much at all. Most of my time is spent at the kennels, and whenever we're shut in together, he reads and I exercise.

We aren't friendly, but we have an unspoken agreement: You leave me alone, I'll leave you alone.

By asking that question, he's broken the agreement, and I'm done staying silent.

"No, everything is not fucking okay. I'm in jail. My club is ready to do me in if I don't get my shit together. I have not one, but two men in this jail who need to meet their maker before I go wherever the fuck I end up going. I'm in this tiny cell with a man I do not know, and a dog that doesn't even look like a fucking dog. And I'm trying to put a bow in the frilly ass dog's hair all because the hottest, most infuriating fucking woman I've ever met told me to, and I would do just about anything to see her smile at me again the way she did earlier today."

Whistling, Gibbs tosses his book aside, swings his legs over the bed, and plants his feet on the floor. "There's a lot of shit to unpack there, big guy."

I rake a hand across the stubble on my scalp as I pace across the cell. "Try being inside my fucking head."

Gibbs is quiet for a moment, as both he and Penny watch me pace back and forth. "I don't know how to help you with your whole being in jail, or the two men meeting their maker, but I'll tell you what I can help you with."

I pause. "What?"

"I can totally do that pretty little dog's bow for you."

This is the most I've heard Gibbs say, and suddenly,

so many things about him begin to fall into place. "You know how to do a bow?"

Gibbs chuckles. "Oh, honey, bless your heart. I can French braid your whole dog if you really want me to. Hand me that comb and a couple of bows, and we'll get her looking so pretty, even that infuriating woman of yours won't recognize her."

Gaydar alarms go off in my head as I hand Gibbs the equipment he needs to help me with Penny.

"This is the most we've ever talked, you and me," I say, watching Gibbs coax Penny a little closer with his hand and a gentle smile.

He grins at me from over his shoulder. "I keep to myself. Only two more days and I'm outta here, and I ain't never comin' back. Guy like me,"—He indicates himself, as if that should mean something to me—"we don't usually do too well here in lockup. Either that, or we do a little too well, if you know what I mean."

I do know what he means.

"Jail isn't exactly LGBTQ friendly," I agree.

He watches me carefully, a tiny lock of Penny's hair pinched between his thumb and forefinger. "And you? Are you LGBTQ friendly?"

"I couldn't care less who you like to fuck, Gibbs. Homophobes are assholes."

Gibbs smiles. "Total assholes."

I can only imagine the fear he's felt, being locked

inside with these inmates. Hell, even with me. I dwarf the poor fucker. But lucky for him, he has the cell all to himself most of the time.

"Ta-da!" Gibbs sings, spinning around and holding Penny out to me as if she's wearing the blue ribbon from the county fair.

Fucking bows. I hate to admit it, but with that stupid ponytail sticking out the top of her tiny little head, her brown eyes look even brighter, making her cute as hell.

"Thanks, man. She looks like she should be in some rich bitch's purse instead of this cell with you and me, but I know Delilah will like it for sure."

Gibbs laughs. "That the gorgeous, infuriating one?"

"The one and only."

Crossing the cell, he takes a seat on his bed, and I sit across from him on mine.

"She know you like her?"

I frown. "I don't like her. She's a fucking employee here. I'm an inmate."

"Mm-hmm," he murmurs, like he's considering those words, but doesn't actually believe them. "So you wanted your dog to have that gay ass bow because…?"

"She's hot. Whatever. I have more important things to worry about, though."

"Those things have anything to do with the two men and the whole meeting their maker business?"

Shit. Sometimes when I get pissed off, I say a little more than I should.

"Yeah. How about we forget that part?"

"Don't worry. I'm not gonna go snitchin' on ya."

I consider that. I don't know this guy from a hole in the ground, but sometimes, you can just tell from one meeting that you can trust someone. Gibbs won't say a damn word. "You know anything about an inmate here named Chad Elscher?"

He presses his lips together in thought. "Never heard of him."

"What about a Henry Tucker?"

That name gets a reaction. "Oh, yeah. That one, I know."

I perk up then, sitting forward on the edge of the bed. "What do you know?"

"I know he's bad news. He spends a lot of time in solitary because of all the fights he gets into. Though, word on the unit is that he sells kiddie porn, including his own kids, so he has to fight a lot. Even in jail, that's a big no-no."

Gibbs doesn't know the half of it.

"How do I find him?"

He thinks for a moment. "Well, he's in the next block over, so the only time we see him is when we get our one hour out in the yard, which you're never there for because you're always down in the kennel with your hot dog lady. But most of the time, Tucker isn't even out there because he's on restriction or in solitary for fighting, so seeing him out is a rare occurrence."

Fuck. This might take more time than I thought.

Seems like I need to be finding time to get out in the yard with the rest of these yahoos until I can pay a little visit to my good friend Henry.

DELILAH

"MOM, you have to hit the camera button on the bottom of the screen," I repeat for the second time since we connected our video call. You'd think after many years of video chatting every Saturday night, she'd have figured it out by now, but here we are again—same issue every week.

"Lilah, honey, I don't see it," her southern voice rambles behind the black screen. "Oh, wait. There it is." Within seconds, her face pops up on the screen with the kitchen in the background. Mom's gray hair is plaited around the crown of her head, and tendrils of curls frame her face. Her tan skin glows against the dark blue floral dress she's wearing, with a chunky beaded necklace. "There's my favorite child."

"I'm your only child, Mom," I remind her with a soft laugh.

"You can still be my favorite."

"Whatever you say." I roll my eyes. "How was the Rainbow gathering?"

"It was groovy. Great music, good people, great vibes. One of the best gatherings they've had in a long while. Moon and Raymond were able to come. It was so great catching up with them. It's been years since they moved on from the commune." She rattles on and on about her friends, giving me every single detail of the conversations they had, down to what they were wearing and what they ate.

"Mom?"

"And then Moon tells me that she and Raymond found this cute little RV park up for sale. But of course, how could they afford that…"

"Mom!"

"What?" she snaps.

"I'm glad you had fun with Moon and Raymond, but you didn't answer my question."

"I didn't hear you ask a question." That's because she didn't even give me a chance to ask it before going off on one of her tangents.

"How did Dad do with his booth? Did they like it?"

"You know your dad has primo weed, honey," she giggles, winking. "But yes, your dad's new strain was a big hit. He sold out the first day."

"Bet he liked that." Dad's newest enterprise since

California legalized marijuana is cultivating it himself for his own personal use, and to help bring in a little money for the upkeep of the camp. A pseudo job, but I'd never call it that to his face. Working for the man and all that.

"He loved it, but you know him. He'd rather smoke it than sell it, but we can't keep the lights on without it."

My parents aren't exactly what you would call "role models." I grew up in a hippie commune with a dozen other families just like mine. The founder, Jeff, had turned his family's old church campground into a mecca for hippies like my parents, who wanted an easy lifestyle without the outside world pressuring them to conform. Each family was assigned a cabin, and everyone took turns helping in the garden, cooking, or doing the chores. After Jeff passed away seven years ago, he left everything to my parents, and they took over as the caretakers, keeping true to their way of life.

"Where is Dad?"

"Outside, playing with his plants. He should be in anytime." Mom's eyes grow wide at something behind me. "Lilah, honey, did you get a new cat?"

Turning, I spy my latest foster fail, Peony. A flame-tipped Siamese that had been living at the rescue for the last year after being found in an abandoned home.

"Sort of." I shrug. "She was floundering, living inside a cage, so I brought her out here as a trial run."

"Trial run, huh? How long has that trial run been exactly?"

"Four months… But she really is doing well out here, Mom. She's really come out of her shell."

"Lilah, honey, you live in a small enough space as it is. You can't just keep moving in animals."

"I know, but I promise, she's it until I find a bigger place." I'd been saving up to put a tiny home on the property, but between the operating expenses for the rescue, and the local zoning board giving me grief about wanting to put something more permanent on a business property, I put my new house on the back burner for the time being.

"How many do you have now?"

"Four…"

"Four? You live in our old van, baby. You barely have enough room for yourself. Four animals are too much."

She's right. There's barely enough room for me, but these animals were extenuating circumstances. Well, that's what I keep telling myself. At least the other three were on the smaller side. Pepper and Salt were two baby bunnies I was still bottle feeding during the night, and Wasabi, a bald parakeet. They need me.

"I'm making it work," I lie with a smile.

"Making it work and making it a home are two different things. What happens when you meet a man? He's going to take one look at that place and run."

"Mom," I groan.

"I'm not getting any younger, baby. Your dad and I want to be grandparents before we get too old." Here we go again—the baby speech.

"I'm twenty-eight. I have time."

"Well, maybe I don't. You need to put yourself out there more."

"Maybe I already have," I blurt out, instantly regretting it when I see how quickly Mom's face lights up with curiosity.

"Tell me everything." She leans forward, propping her elbows up on the table and resting her chin in her hands, like she's my best gal pal, and I'm about to dish out the juiciest gossip on a reality TV show.

"There's not a lot to tell, Mom. It's new."

"Well, what's he like? What does he do for a living?"

"He's, uh, um...," I stammer. "It's a bit complicated."

Her face falls. "He's not married, is he?"

"Mom, no. Absolutely not." Shit. I don't know that for sure. He very well could be. It's not like that's written in his case file. He could have an entire family that I have no idea exists, and he's just flirting with me because I'm there. What in the hell am I doing? "His name is Rhett."

"Rhett," she repeats slowly. "I like it. It's a strong name. How did you meet him?"

"He's a volunteer with one of my outreach programs." Or participant, but now isn't the time to mention that he's actually an inmate. She doesn't need all the details... yet. "I've been training him."

"Training? Is that what kids call sex these days?" she snickers.

"Oh. My. God. Mom, no. We're not talking about sex. I'm training him for work. Like I said, it's still new. I'm not even sure it's going to get off the ground." Or out of the jail. If I could facepalm myself without alerting Mom, I would. It sounds so ridiculous, talking about him like he's my boyfriend, because he's not, and he never will be.

"New or not, it's good to see you dipping your toes into the water, baby. I say go for it. Let your freak flag fly and see what happens."

I pinch the bridge of my nose. I had definitely made a mistake telling her about Rhett Darby and our non-existent relationship.

"Don't act like that. This is the first guy you've brought up since, oh... what was that boy's name? You know, the one with the crooked teeth and big glasses?" She mimics with her hands, trying to give me visual aids for what she's trying to explain.

"Robert Burnside? Mom, that was fifteen years ago. I was thirteen. How do you even remember that?"

"A mother never forgets her little girl's first love."

"You're ridiculous." He wasn't my first love. He was the boy who chased me around the commune, calling me names and throwing mud at me. The guy was a pest. "I've dated plenty of other guys since then. I'm not a nun, Mom." Plenty, meaning a grand total of three. After being dumped by the guy I had dated all throughout college three weeks before graduation and moving in together via an email, I realized then and there that maybe it was time I lived life for myself and figure out what I wanted to do. Turns out, my path was running an animal rescue and acquiring massive amounts of debt while living in my parent's old van. #lifegoals?

"None of which you've ever introduced to your dad and I, honey. If they aren't meet the parents' material, do they really count?"

"Seriously, I don't have time to date." Well, in Rhett's case, I have all the time in the world. You know, jail and all that. A loud crash from behind Mom pulls her attention away from the screen. "What's that?" she asks behind her.

Dad's muffled voice replies through the background, "My new strain. I crossed White Widow and Sour Diesel. More relaxing and twice the energy. It's going to be a hit with the local college kids during exam week."

"You didn't answer me. Why is it in the house?"

"One of the kids broke out a window in the greenhouse, and I didn't want them to get too cold tonight. I have twelve more pots outside."

"You are not bringing those in this house." They argue for a bit before Dad notices me on the screen.

"Why didn't you tell me Delilah called? Hi, honey!" He steps closer to the screen and shoves a small pot of baby marijuana plants into the camera's lens, taking up the whole screen. "Look at my new plants."

"They look great, Dad," I lie. The plants move out of the camera's view and are replaced by my dad's face. His big, bushy beard is more peppery than the last time we'd chatted. But being almost sixty years old, it's a surprise he's not already a cotton top.

"You look tired. Do I need to send you something to relax?"

I wipe my hand across my face. "It's not legal here, Dad. You know that." Not that I would play puff puff pass. I tried it a few times, but it really wasn't for me.

"It should be legal everywhere!" he exclaims, proceeding to go on a tirade about how the man is pulling us all down, and that the weed should be free to the people. I listen for fifteen minutes as he argues his points to a non-existent lecture room. Mom adds in her own points as he paces between her in the kitchen.

"Hey, I've gotta go. I need to do food and water checks before I head to bed." Dad just continues on. "Hey, Mom! Dad! I need to log off. Can you still hear me?"

Neither one of them notices as I shut the lid to my laptop and sigh out loud. Why couldn't I have been born into a normal family?

STONEFACE

NEVER IN MY WILDEST, most fucked-up dreams would I ever have imagined I'd be excited about showing off a hair bow to a woman. And if any one of these motherfuckers knew it, I'd likely be a dead man.

Nevertheless, Penny looks like she belongs on some reality TV show for dogs, and I can't wait to see Delilah's reaction.

From the corner of my eye, I watch Elscher as he goes about his training with his own dog, but I keep my gaze focused toward the door, waiting to see those round hips and gorgeous eyes come walking through.

Not good, hombre, I think to myself. But just as quickly as the thought floats through my head, I shove it away and perk up when Delilah walks in.

I continue working with Penny, squatting low to the ground as I teach her to roll over. She's nearly got the trick nailed, which doesn't surprise me, seeing as I'm pretty sure she's a genius of the K9 variety.

Penny does a perfect rollover, just as I see one of the guards flirting it up with Delilah. He leans in close, his face right near her ear. If he gets any closer, I'll rip his fucking lips off and feed them to my dog.

Delilah throws her head back and laughs at whatever the douche fucker says, but then walks away. Why does it piss me off so much that she's still laughing?

"Well, hello, Penny," she sings as she draws closer. My instinct to grab her and yank her to me grows stronger as I glare over her shoulder at the guard, who is now staring at her ass. "Oh, wow! Mr. Darby, her hair is incredible."

I smile. "Thanks. Those bows are a bitch, but we figured it out."

"His celly did it, Miss Lilah," Buddy outs me. "Stone-Face broke all the bows but one."

I turn and throw a dog treat at him. "Mind your own business, fucker. Friends don't rat friends out."

Buddy giggles and focuses back on his dog.

When I turn back, Delilah is still crouched down, petting Penny, but her eyes are on me. There's something there, in her expression, that makes my heart rate soar. A softness, a fondness, and it's directed right at me.

"Thought you could get one over on me, did you, Mr. Darby?"

Shrugging, I chuckle.

"Your trainer is kinda naughty, isn't he, Penny?"

Penny lets out an excited yip of agreement and flops on the ground to roll over.

Delilah giggles and stands, muttering something about rule number four before she wanders away, making brief visits to each of the other inmates.

Once she's made her way around the room once, and in some cases, returning to a couple of the inmates twice —I know this, because I counted—she returns to me.

"Hey, I've got a bunch of obstacle course equipment I need to pull out for today's training. Can you come give me a hand?"

Mr. Dead-if-he-flirts-with-her-again overhears her request. "I'll help."

Delilah smiles at the guard and shakes her head. I can't help but do an internal fist pump when I see that her smile doesn't quite reach her eyes. "The more the inmates help, the more it helps with being rehabilitated. They need to fully immerse themselves into the program."

The guard studies her for a moment, then turns his attention to me. "You help her carry shit. Leave the door open. If I hear so much as a fucking peep out of you, I'll throw you in solitary indefinitely. We clear?"

I try to hold back my sneer, but it's pointless. I used to be the master of controlling my facial features. It's one of the reasons I'd gotten the name StoneFace back when I was just a prospect.

Since meeting Delilah and Penny, I was losing my touch.

"He understands," Delilah assures him as she motions for me to follow her.

The utility closet is on the far side of the massive room, which means I get to watch her ass sway in those bell-bottom jeans for the entire walk.

Heat builds inside my pants. At this point, I've been in lockup for a couple of months, and I haven't even seen another woman. No sex. No porn. No five minutes alone to even take matters into my own hands, in the very literal sense.

Fucking hell.

Delilah opens the door and steps inside. "So, this side of the room here is all of our equipment. We need to pull it all out, and then I'll get everyone to help us set it up." She steps up to a tall shelf and reaches for a pile of small orange pylons.

As she pops up on her toes and lifts her hand, I swallow at the sight of her creamy smooth skin. I'd give anything to run my fingertips across that tiny patch of skin, straight to the button right below it.

Suddenly, the whole shelf begins to wobble, and Delilah's balance wavers. She grabs onto the shelf for support—a dangerous move.

Rushing forward, I reach above her and grab onto the medicine ball that had almost dropped onto her head and steady the shelf. As my front meets her back, Delilah lets out a shocked gasp and spins around.

My hand is still up high, holding the ball in place on the shelf. My chest is now pressed against her breasts, feeling them rise and fall with every breath she draws in. Her eyes are wide and innocent as she gapes up at me, her lips parted in surprise. And, if I'm not mistaken, desire.

A desire that rivals my own.

Allowing the ball to roll into my hand, I remove it from the shelf and drop it to the floor beside me. Once my hand is free, I spear it up into the hair at the nape of her neck, place my other hand on the perfect curve of her ample hip, and kiss her.

Her lips are luscious and warm, and so fucking soft, my knees start to wobble.

She tastes of apples and cinnamon, and her hair is everywhere, surrounding me. I need more, want more, so I take more.

Drawing her closer, I press her against me and deepen our scorching hot kiss while trailing my fingers down her side until the palm of my hand is cupping her ass.

Suddenly, unexpectedly, Delilah tears her lips from mine and pushes her body back against the shelf, putting as much distance between us as physically possible. Her eyes are wide and shocked and absolutely terrified.

The tips of her fingers come up to touch her slightly swollen lips. "No," she whispers. "No, no, no. We can't, Rhett."

She pushes against me as she speaks, her words erupting from her mouth, but doing very little to diminish my need for her.

"We can't," she repeats, pushing past me to collect a large red and yellow tunnel. "Let's get this stuff and get set up. Can you grab that box horse over in the corner and put it at the far side of the course?"

She's still talking as she exits the closet, leaving me alone with my burning lips and my very prominent hard-on.

Fuck. That was stupid. I never should've kissed her like that. I'm lucky she didn't scream bloody murder and run into the arms of that pussy ass guard out there.

Pissed off, and even more sexually frustrated than I was before, I grab the box horse and lift it, along with its base, and take it to the part of the main room she'd indicated.

Delilah is busy scurrying in and out of the closet, bringing out various tunnels and pylons.

When I return to the closet, I grab the large, dog-sized teeter-totter and make my way toward the door.

"Rhett?" Delilah calls from behind me.

I turn, just as her lips crash into mine. Her fingertips claw at my arms, drawing me closer, and I don't resist at all. Instead, I drop the teeter-totter, ignoring the clatter it makes as it hits the floor, and press her against the wall, my lips moving with hers in perfect, heated harmony.

"Miss Walker?" the guard calls out, his footsteps drawing nearer.

Reluctantly, I tear away from Delilah and take a step back, just as he steps into the room. "Everything okay? I heard a bang."

He eyes me with suspicion.

"Yeah," she says, her voice more air than sound. "Yeah. I, uh... I knocked over the teeter-totter, and Mr. Darby is just giving me a hand."

Her hair's a mess, her chest heaving, and her lips are perfectly swollen, but this jackass doesn't even notice. Instead, he nods and goes back to what he was doing.

"Let's get this stuff out there before we get into trouble, shall we?"

She doesn't look at me again, but that's okay, because she'd given something to me when she gave me that kiss. She'd given me herself. If only I could be the man to keep her.

DELILAH

I KISSED HIM. *Oh. My. God.* I'd actually freaking kissed him. What the hell was I thinking? Going into that closet was a huge mistake. I never should've asked him to help me. I should've never put myself into that situation.

Trying to push the delicious memory from my mind, I move to the back of the rescue, to where the bathroom is. Living in a van means that I'm without certain amenities, hence why I do the majority of my personal hygiene routine in the back of Austin Animal Rescue headquarters.

I twist the knob and set the water to the heat level I prefer. *And it still wouldn't be as hot as that kiss.*

Damn it, Delilah. Snap your ass out of it. He's in jail.

I step into the shower and stand with my face under the spray of water.

But that kiss. A frozen moment in time, with his demanding lips devouring mine. His strong fingers pulling me to him like he wanted me to climb inside of him and make myself at home.

It felt like it was straight out of one of those dark romance movies where the bad guy gets the innocent girl. But after that, I no longer feel innocent. I feel desired and wanton, and so fucking turned on. I feel different in a way I can't even explain.

"No. It was just a kiss," I say out loud, my voice dulled under the shower.

He's just a man. A man who had kissed me like I was his only source of oxygen, and his lungs were on the verge of collapse. It may have been just a kiss to him, but to me, it was so much more.

Turning my back into the cascading water, I tip my head back, feeling like every drop is electric. Charged. It runs down my body, tiny streams that feel like fingers racing along my curves. His fingers—Rhett's fingers.

Unable to fight it, I moan softly and allow my imagination to carry me away.

I imagine him here in the shower with me right now. God, he's so fucking muscular. I'd learned what it feels like to have his body pressed against mine earlier, and it wasn't long enough. I want to feel that again. I want to take it all the way. I need him to go all the way with me.

My fingertips run around the edges of my nipples,

excitement racing along my spine as I imagine Rhett's tongue doing the same. I imagine it flicking the hard bud there, and his lips pressing butterfly soft kisses all around. I imagine his teeth nipping at each one as his eyes bore into mine with unadulterated need.

"Jesus," I whisper, struggling to draw air into my lungs. If I can get this excited with the imaginary Rhett, imagine how my body would respond to the real one.

I move my fingertips down a little lower, tracing the heavy curve of my breast, and glide down along the center of my belly, trailing across my belly button and lower still.

When I reach my center, I slowly dip my finger between my folds and shiver as I imagine Rhett touching me this way. I can feel him, smell him, and I want more than anything to have him here in this shower with me.

Slowly, gently, I roll my swollen nub beneath the wet tip of my finger and moan. I take my time rolling and rubbing, my hips moving in a rhythm. It's been so long since I've been touched, and no one like Rhett Darby has ever touched me—until today.

Need coils inside of me, but my fingers are no longer providing the release I so desperately need.

Reaching up, I grab the nozzle above me and pull it from its cradle. I adjust the spray, finding one with more pressure, and position myself with my foot up on the edge of the tub as I lower the shower head. The massaging spray hits my clit, sending my head falling back.

"Oh, God." I think about Rhett, imagining his face buried between my legs, his tongue dancing and swirling around my clit. I imagine him lapping at me like a starving man.

A cold white heat builds beneath his imaginary tongue. My knees begin to quiver, and then I erupt.

Quaking, I ride the steady stream of water, releasing every bit of pent-up need I have inside. I'm alone in the building, and for that, I'm thankful, because I can't control my pleasure.

My chest heaves and my heart races as I float back down to reality.

Jesus Christ, I needed that.

I give myself a moment to catch my breath and then place the shower head back in its place.

I've come to a decision. I have a new rule—rule five. Fuck all the rules. I want this. I want him. And if I have to wait for him to get out, I'll fucking do it.

STONEFACE

YARD TIME in jail is hard to come by most days. Everyone gets a bit of time outside seven days a week, but my schedule has been so busy with Buddy and the animal rehabilitation program, I rarely get to enjoy it.

This is the first time in almost a month I've stepped foot outside the inner walls of the prison. The yard itself isn't much to brag on. A grassy area that's mostly trampled on and covered in cigarette butts. A paved area around two net-less basketball hoops that hang from matching rusty looking metal poles. There are two picnic tables and a row of benches along the side of the fenced area. Above us, guards wander a walkway atop the brick wall, their eyes scanning every detail of our brief encounter with the great outdoors, and each other.

The fresh air feels amazing as it fills my lungs. I could

lie out here, soaking up the sun's rays for hours, but there's another reason I came out here today.

Scanning every single face in the crowd, my eyes search for Henry Tucker. It had been almost a year since I'd laid eyes on him, but you never forget the face of the man who had nearly destroyed the lives of people you love.

Henry Tucker is a bad man. Very bad. And the fact that his black heart still beats needs to be rectified immediately.

And then I see him.

Across the yard, his back leaning against the brick wall, Tucker scans the crowd as well. Guys like him don't do too good in jail. This might be a place full of criminals, but woman beaters and child molesters are just as much outcasts here as they are on the outside.

Henry Tucker is both those things.

Standing, I double check the small of my back, reassuring myself that the shiv I'd gotten from the inmate as a gift from Judge is still there. The guards are true sentinels, their eyes never wavering from the yard below them.

"Wanna play basketball?" Buddy asks, coming up to me with a ball with barely any air in it.

I peel my eyes away from Tucker, just long enough to address my friend. "Not today, Buddy. Just want to enjoy the sunshine."

"Okay," he says, his voice filled with disappointment.

Normally, I would feel kind of bad for rejecting him, but right now, all I can think about is how the fuck I'm gonna pull this off without being caught?

I can't get caught, not for this. I still have Elscher to take care of. After both of these motherfuckers are gone, I don't care what the hell happens to me, but it can't happen until I get them both.

One at a time, asshole.

Cool and collected, I walk along the side of the yard, my brain churning with different ways to do this.

And then it happens.

I don't hear the argument that starts it all, and I don't know either of the men involved. All I know is that one black guy throws a killer punch, hitting a large white guy square in the jaw. The white guy goes soaring through the air and lands on his ass, bouncing twice before jumping to his feet and back in the fight.

That's all it takes. Suddenly, everyone in the yard is fighting. The sound of flesh on flesh and groans of exertion, followed by roars of pain and anger fill the air.

The guards are on their loudspeakers, but I don't pause to listen. Instead, my head whips around to locate Buddy. He's right where I'd left him, looking shocked, but standing far enough away from the melee to be safe. Just where I want him.

In a move so fast, I know the cameras won't catch it, I

snatch the shiv from the back of my pants and palm it in a way that conceals it behind my arm.

Making my way toward Henry Tucker, I knock out anyone that comes at me. One punch and they're down, no exceptions.

And then I'm there. I want to tell him it's about to happen. I want to tell him this is for Lindsey and her unborn baby. For his own kids, who he'd traumatized nearly beyond repair. I want to watch the life drain from his eyes as he realizes exactly who I am and what I've done.

But there's no time. The cameras are watching. The guards are coming.

Grabbing Tucker by the shoulder, I whip him around until we're nose to nose.

Recognition flashes in his eyes, quickly followed by fear.

With lightning-fast strikes, I slam the shiv into his torso once, twice, three times. His mouth opens in shock, but no sound comes out. At least not one I can hear amongst the commotion.

I stab at him six more times, then one for good measure. That tenth one is when I stop, pulling away, leaving the shiv exactly where it belongs, deep inside the belly of the beast.

Tucker falls to the ground, his eyes wide with terror,

his heart pumping the last of his life's blood out onto the patchy grass.

I don't stick around long enough to find out what happens next. Instead, I throw myself back into the fray, throwing elbows and fists, making sure to allow a few to land on me as well. There's no question in my mind that Henry Tucker is dead, and I need an alibi.

By the time the whistles are blowing, guards are storming into the yard in full riot gear, tear gas filling the space, causing my eyes to water and burn.

"On the ground!" they scream. All of them are shouting, all of them sounding equal parts angry and nervous. I don't blame them. Pissed off inmates outnumber them by about ten to one, but most of us obey.

I don't argue or put up a fight. I drop to my knees, put my hands behind my head, and lay down on my belly as instructed. I stay that way for several minutes as everyone around me argues with the guards, pleading their innocence.

Any second now, they're gonna discover Tucker's body.

And that, my friends, is fucking justice.

DELILAH

THERE'S something off in the air when I arrive back at the jail. I could feel it as soon as I stepped outside. Its inky weirdness spread all over me when I stepped inside the building, only to find the sheriff speaking with Jessica. Both of them turn to me when I make my way toward them.

"Miss Walker." The sheriff smiles, approaching me with his hand extended. "It's so nice to make your acquaintance in person." His heavy southern accent is loaded with fake sincerity and charm.

"To what do I owe this pleasure, Sheriff?" I'd been here for months now, and most of that time, I had been trying to get an audience with his highness, but he'd been dodging my calls and never returning my messages.

"Just offering a friendly 'hello' to you, that's all."

I raise my brow. The weirdness from outside is spreading inside.

"If you have some free time, I'd love to sit down and chat with you. I've been trying to get onto your appointment calendar, but your secretary said you were booked solid."

"Yes, I am," he drawls.

"Well, you don't seem to be tied down right now. Do you have time for a quick chat?"

"I wish I did, Miss Walker, but I'm on my way out for the day. Meetings with the mayor and governor, you see." He offers me a cocky grin. "Try giving Dolores that call again."

Because, of course, he had big meetings. What do you want to bet these meetings will be taking place on a golf course with a case of beer being lugged around by their own personal caddy?

He dips his hat to the both of us before heading out of the door, without so much as a second glance. I pivot to Jessica, who stands sternly, and uneasily silent.

"Everything okay?" I inquire.

"Fine. Your class will be a bit smaller today."

"Why's that?"

"Nothing for you to be concerned about."

"I think I have a right to know where my animals are, Jessica."

"All the dogs are in their kennels.

"Okay?"

A voice calls out over the radio on her shoulder. Leaning into it, she answers back. "I have to go. You know the way to the kennels." She takes off in the opposite direction of the kennels with fire, leaving a trail from her black leather boots.

First, the sheriff showing up. Now, Jessica not giving me the time of day. What's next?

Getting to the kennel areas, I realize I should have never asked that question. When Jessica said small class, I had no idea she meant over half the participants would be missing, including Rhett and Buddy. Penelope and Rocco are where they should be in their kennels, but the two men are missing, along with so many others. Even Chad is nowhere to be seen, though his absence is a welcome one.

What's happened? Was there an illness going through the cell blocks? So many scenarios explaining his—I mean, *their* absences, run through my mind. The room seems so empty without *him—them!* God. I have Rhett on my mind. *You did last night too, and the night before that.* I have a problem. A big one named Rhett hot-as-sin Darby.

Welp, if today is going to be weird, I best get on with it.

After checking on all the animals in their kennels, and working with those present for today's session for more than two hours, a few more of the participants trickle into the room, including Chad. *Can't catch a break, can I?*

He takes one look at me and beelines himself over, completely ignoring Missy's cries for his attention. The huge smile on his face would be the twisted mirror version of the grimace on mine.

"Miss me?"

Like a fucking heart attack. The last place I want to be is anywhere he is.

"You don't have to answer, because I know you did."

I wasn't planning on answering that. If I could pretend he didn't exist at all, I'd be doing that instead of trying to figure out how I'm going to get out of this. Normally, I could rely on Rhett or Buddy to bail me out, but my pseudo-security team is missing in action.

"Been waiting to see you to tell you the good news. My lawyer says I'm going to be a free man as soon as next week."

"That so?" I reply.

Our legal system never fails to confound me. Chad Elscher is a convicted murderer, serving a life sentence. How is it possible that he's going to get out? I don't know the particulars of his exact case, but murderers with life sentences aren't often released as easily as he's making the process out to be.

"Yeah," he continues. I'm not really sure if he's oblivious to my uncaring attitude or he just doesn't give a shit. "I was just a kid when all that shit happened, but I'm a grown man now with years of good behavior. They'll see that I've changed. My lawyer said it would be good if I could ask you to write a recommendation for me? About how good I've been with Missy?"

"Maybe," I say, though there's no way in hell I will ever write that letter. "Speaking of Missy, maybe you should go check on her. She's been barking since you walked into the room."

"She's fine, Delilah." Tilting his head to the side, he frowns. "It's not every day that I get you alone like this, you know. You always seem to have a fan club hovering around you."

I take my chance to try to change the subject. "Where is everyone? Did something happen?"

"Rumor has it some old pedophile got shanked in a yard fight. Happened when I was meeting with my lawyer, so I don't know all the details." The way he talks about someone being murdered so nonchalantly throws me off balance. For a reformed murderer—killer of another person—it doesn't seem to faze him at all.

My stomach drops. Yard fights meant lockdowns. Buddy and Rhett couldn't have been involved, could they? "Did anyone else get hurt? Do they know who did it? Is that where Buddy is? Rhett?"

Chad's entire body stiffens. "How the fuck should I know?" His beady eyes narrow and his lip curls. "Why do you even care? They're inmates. You've been spending way too much time with that big fucker. You barely even talk to me anymore."

I don't like the way he's looking at me right now. Possessive. Obsessed, even. "They're a part of my program, Chad. I'm simply concerned about them."

"Looks like you're a little more than concerned, if you ask me. The big motherfucker hovers around you like a lost puppy, Delilah. I don't like that."

"He's new," I reply. "I'm showing him the ropes." Feeling infinitely more uncomfortable now, I scan the room for a guard, but just like there are less inmates today, there are also less guards. And there are none to be seen at the moment.

"Whatever," Chad says, waving his hand and forcing a smile onto his face. "Forget them. What about you, though? What do you say you and me go out once I'm out of here?"

I'd rather him punch me in the face. "Go out? Like, on a date?"

His smile grows wider. "Yeah. Dinner, dancing, maybe a couple of beers. Would be fun."

My insides twist and turn just thinking of him being free and out of jail. What does that mean for the rest of the world? This man is a monster. How can they just let him out?

"I appreciate the offer, Chad, but I don't think that's a

very good idea." I force myself to smile while using a gentle tone, praying he'll make this easy on me. But something terrifying flashes in the depths of his eyes, and I know then he won't let that happen.

His jaw sets, hard as stone. "Why not?"

Shit. Why not?

Do I tell him that I have a boyfriend? Or that I'm a lesbian, maybe?

"I really don't date," I lie, my heart racing as I scan the room again, desperate for a guard to come along.

Chad's eyes are narrowed to angry slits now. "You mean, you don't date men like me—criminals."

I raise a hand and take a step back, angling myself away from the wall and into the open, near some of the other inmates. "That's not what I said."

Like magic, the anger evaporates from his face and is replaced with hope and happiness. "We'd have a lot of fun, Delilah. It's been forever since I've been on a date, but I promise I'll show you a good time. We could go dancing, or to a movie. Whatever you want, we can do."

Jesus Christ. Where are the fucking guards?

"Chad, I'm sorry, but I'm not interested," I say, finally managing to slip past him. "I do appreciate the offer. Now, if you'll excuse me, I'm about to start teaching an obedience class."

Whipping around, I speed walk my way toward the

kennel and the tiny closet where I keep some of my supplies. I can feel Chad's frustrated glare burning holes in my back, but that had ended a lot better than it could have.

Arriving at the closet, I open the door and step inside, my chest heaving as my heart threatens to pump itself right out of it at rocket speed. Chad had never made it a secret that he was interested, but if I'm honest, most of these inmates are interested. Not because I'm attractive or desirable, or a great catch, but because I have tits and a vagina, and they're locked up with a bunch of other men.

"Everything okay?"

Letting out a yelp of surprise, I press my hand to my chest and gape at the guard standing just a few feet away.

"Jeepers! You scared the bejesus out of me!"

The guard stifles a laugh. "Sorry, ma'am."

"Where were you? I was looking for a guard a few minutes ago."

He frowns. "I was just inside the kennel. A couple of the inmates' argument was getting a little heated. Thought I was gonna have to break up a fight. I'm here now, though. What did you need?"

I look around the corner and watch as Chad pats Missy on top of her head and puts her into another sit, stay pose.

"Nothing," I say. "Just making sure someone was around."

I'd hate to report what had just happened with Chad to the guard. Nothing had actually happened, if I really think about it. He made a pass at me. I rejected. He pushed a bit. I walked away. End of story. And hopefully, the end of Chad's obsession.

STONEFACE

FORTY-EIGHT HOURS in solitary confinement is hell when your brain is all fucked up with contradicting thoughts of a beautiful woman you can't get out of your head, putting an end to one man's life, and desperately needing to put an end to another's.

"Where have you guys been? It's been two days!" Delilah cries, rushing over as Buddy and I are led into the kennels.

"We were in big trouble," Buddy tells her, but he keeps walking toward the kennel, eager to be reunited with Rocco.

Delilah watches him go, then looks at me with about a million questions in her eyes.

"We were on vacation," I say. "But instead of some sandy beach somewhere, we opted for a six by eight cell, where they serve us mushy food and keep us from talking to anyone else with a pulse."

Delilah's eyes grow wide. "Are you okay, though?"

We make our way through the massive room toward the kennel area, where poor Penny has been locked up in her own form of solitary. "I'm fine. Buddy's fine. They locked down everyone that was in the yard the other day. Dude got shanked, and they were trying to figure out who did it."

"Did they?" she asks. "Figure it out?"

Shrugging, I hold the gate open for her, motioning for her to step inside. "Fuck if I know. They let us out, and that's all I gave a shit about."

Penny sees us coming, and her yips of excitement pierce the air, as well as my eardrums, but I'm so fucking happy to see her, I don't even care. "Hey, little lady," I coo, popping open the door on her kennel and watching as she comes barreling out, her whole ass getting into the effort of wagging her tail. "Look at you." I lean down to pick up the vibrating ball of fluff, but she dodges my hand and continues to bounce all around me like an absolute lunatic.

I chuckle, attempting to pick her up three more times, and then finally give up. Careful not to squash her, I lower myself to the ground and hold my arms out.

Penny barrels onto my lap, her tiny, mile-long tongue

licking me anywhere and everywhere she can reach. "Did you miss me?"

Delilah grabs a milk crate and pulls it closer. Taking a seat across from me, her face splits into a wide, radiant smile. "I think it's safe to say, she did."

I smile, nuzzling Penny, and then refocus my attention on Delilah. "Did you?"

Delilah's face freezes in an instant, her smile fading. I'd caught her off guard. Though I hate to see her uncomfortable at all, it's nice to know that my presence affects her just as much as hers does mine.

After a moment, her face grows serious, and I know that our lighthearted moment is no longer. "Why did you steal that police car?"

Well, shit.

Her question doesn't have a simple answer, but considering she asked at all, I'm willing to bet she knows that.

This is a pivotal moment for us. I can feel it, and I know she can feel it too.

No matter what happens, in every moment of our lives, we always have two choices. We can face our fears or uncertainties by moving forward, or we can stay in the place we're at by not bothering to take a step at all.

If I'm to have anything with Delilah, I need to take that fucking first step.

"I needed to be sent here," I admit after an extremely long pause.

"Here," she repeats. "Like, to Travis County Jail?"

I nod.

Her nose wrinkles with confusion. "Why on earth would you want to come here?"

One quick glance around tells me we're as alone as we are ever going to get in jail. The guard that likes to flirt with her is on the far side of the massive room, but he can't hear what we're saying. The kennel itself is empty, except for us. Even Buddy had collected Rocco and gone right out to the training area, excited to finally be back with his friend.

This is it. Telling Delilah this will either make or break our relationship.

"There's a man here that needs to die."

Her eyes never waver from mine, but I hear her breath catch in her throat.

"Why? What man?"

I force myself to hold her gaze as I say, "The man that killed my sister."

Closing her eyes, she swallows hard. We stay that way for several minutes. Her with her eyes closed, me with my eyes on her.

Finally, she looks me in the eye and scoots her milk crate closer. "You had a sister?"

A breath of dread I hadn't even realized I'd been

holding evacuates my lungs. If she hasn't run away screaming by now, I doubt she will now.

"Twin sister. I was older by seven minutes, and I reminded her of that all the time."

The way she's watching me right now, with her eyes so soft and understanding, is like a dagger to my soul. Nobody has ever looked at me that way. I'm not even worthy of her understanding, but fuck me, I crave it almost as much as I crave her.

I go back to petting Penny, who is now curled up on my lap, unable to meet Delilah's caring gaze. "She was murdered by an inmate here," I continue.

Penny's eyes fall closed as I run my thick, tattooed fingers through her hair. She's my distraction from the reality of the pain in my heart. She's grounding me, making this easier to share with Delilah.

"I've never told anyone this before," I confess.

"Never?"

"No."

"Sounds like a lot to carry all on your own," she notes, her voice sincere.

My jaw tightens as I feel a lump growing in my throat. My heart aches, not used to being able to feel this pain.

"What was her name?"

It's hard to force her name from my throat and out of my mouth, but I manage to say, "R-Reba."

I haven't said my sister's name out loud in almost eighteen years. It wasn't because she was a secret, or that I was trying to forget. It was because the very thought of what had happened to her had become my soul reason for still fucking breathing.

I was going to get revenge on the people who had murdered her.

"Rhett and Reba," Delilah vocalizes with a smile. "I like it."

I tip up the corner of my lips in a half-assed smile. "My momma wanted our names to match."

Delilah considers that. "Where's your momma now?"

"Gone." I keep my gaze on Penny, because if I look anywhere else right now, I might break apart. "She wasn't around much when we were growing up. Worked several jobs just to pay the bills. She died just a couple of months before Reba. My old man died of a heart attack when I was just a kid."

Her hand rests on top of mine. It's so tiny and warm, creamy smooth on top of my rough tattooed skin. She gives it a tender squeeze. "I'm so sorry, Rhett."

"No touching!" the guard hollers from the other side of the room.

She rips her hand from mine, but the ghost of her sweet touch still lingers. The guard is walking toward us, and our moment of solitude is about to come to an end.

"She wouldn't want you to live like this," Delilah

says, dipping her head to meet my eyes. She stares at me a beat before continuing. "Your momma or your sister. They wouldn't want you to live your entire life to avenge her death. That's not living."

My jaw hardens, but I hold her gaze. "That fucker killed my sister. He fucking tortured her. She didn't die easily, and he won't either. I'll make sure he feels the same pain and terror he caused her."

Pressing her lips together, she leans forward, lowering her voice so the approaching guard doesn't hear. "Do you think Reba would want this pain on your soul? Do you think she would want you to be in jail for the rest of your life, all because you were avenging her death?"

My chest grows tight, and I try to release the scowl I know is showing on my face.

"I know you don't want to hear this, Rhett, but your sister and your momma wouldn't want this. They would want you to live. To have a happy life. Your sister didn't get a chance to have that. You need to be living a life for yourself *and* for her. That's what she would want."

The guard approaches then. "A little more distance," he orders, motioning for Delilah to push her milk crate farther away.

I can't help but smirk when she rolls her eyes and makes a show of dragging the crate a few inches away and plopping her ass back down on it. "Like this?"

The guard's jaw pops, and he nods before moving just a few feet away to lean against the wall, his eyes on the whole room, but his ears most definitely on our conversation.

Delilah ignores him. "Your sister's memory shouldn't cause you pain. It does because you're focusing on her death. And I didn't know the girl, but I am one, so I'm willing to bet that Reba would hate that for you. She would want you to remember the good stuff from when she was alive. Her life may have been short, but her death was just one terrible moment amongst so many wonderful ones. Those are what you should focus on."

I hate her words, but I love that she has the courage to say them. And I know that at least part of what she's saying is right. Reba would kick my ass if she knew I never told people about her. Or, at least, she'd try to.

Just then, Elscher wanders into the kennel and glares as he wanders past us.

As much as I think Delilah is right, I don't know how to move on and be happy as long as that fucker is still drawing air into his lungs. Reba would be pissed, but I can't let this shit go. I can't let him live another day while my sister is in the ground.

DELILAH

LEAVING THE JAIL, my mind plays back my conversation with Rhett over and over again.

He'd trusted me with something today that he had never told anyone before. That means something to me, just as I know it meant something to him, too. The weight of what he'd revealed was so very heavy. I don't know how he's shouldered it alone for so long. And what did it mean that he'd shared it with me? And why did it feel like that talk had changed absolutely everything?

Because it's Rhett.

It wasn't playful flirting or innuendos, but a real and deep conversation. The first one we've had since we met. He'd trusted me with that. He'd given me a piece of himself that only I could lay claim to.

Rhett Darby is a hard man. He rarely smiles, doesn't

say much, and considering the fact that he's in jail, he doesn't necessarily always do what's right in the eyes of society, but I know there's a good man there.

Under all that pain, anger, and guilt, love and goodness still reside. He may not see it, but the way he treats Buddy shows me it's there. After today, I have zero doubts that maybe the feelings I've been developing for him could mean something. That we could have a chance. That he may feel the same way about me.

My mind swirls as I go through the motions of my evening, analyzing every detail of our relationship and our talk. I go to the rescue and take a shower, then head to the van and cook myself up a veggie burger on my portable grill.

It's not until I've sat down with my burger and sweet potato fries that I realize Rhett had said his sister was murdered, but he'd never told me by who, or even how.

I glance at my MacBook lying on the bed. Should I look it up? Surely there's something about it online.

Guilt washes over me for even considering the notion. If he had wanted me to know, he would've told me. Right? A nagging sensation to find out for myself pokes and prods at me until I make a snap decision. I have to know.

Snatching up my computer, I flop down on the bed, open it up, and click on the browser icon. As soon as the

Google search page loads, I enter the words "Reba Darby murder."

Instantly, a series of links pop up. The first result is an obituary listing from a funeral home in Alabama, dated nearly eighteen years ago. I click the link, and a photo pops up at the top of the screen of his sister.

Her features are so different from Rhett's. Feminine and perfectly proportioned. You'd never guess they were related, unless you looked at her eyes. Her eyes are identical to her twin brother's. A deep hazel with flecks of green.

I stare at that photo for a few moments, pain tearing at my heart for this poor young girl who never had a chance to be a woman. And she would have been a beautiful one.

Scrolling down, I scan the brief obituary.

She was only eighteen years old when her life was cut short. My heart breaks for her and her brother. And the names of the people who had died before her... Rhett was all she still had in the world. Her other half, and the piece he's still missing.

I've read stories about the connection that twins sometimes have with each other. How they can feel each other's pain, and sometimes intuitively know what the other is thinking or feeling. It makes me wonder if it had been that way for Rhett and Reba.

Clicking on the tribute page, I find a few comments

from fellow classmates, each one more heartbreaking than the next, but it's something at the bottom of the page that draws my attention—a slideshow of photos. Pictures of her and her brother as children fill the first few minutes as a song takes place in the background. Just the two of them smiling together or playing. Not one of the photos include anyone else.

My family may not be what you would call conventional by any definition of the term, but we were happy, and we were always together. Our home was, and still is, filled with love, hippies, and pot smoke, but it was still a home. I still had my parents.

I can't imagine growing up the way they did. Alone. Their mom always working, their dad just a faint memory.

Neither one of them could've known what a real loving family was, and losing Reba had broken the only tie he had to anyone. It had left him alone.

A tear slips down my cheek as I watch the pictures change every few seconds. The last one nearly shatters me to my soul.

In it, Reba stands next to him in a long, formal dress, beaming from ear to ear, and a smaller, younger version of Rhett stands stoically next to her in his military uniform. You can see how much they loved each other in the color image. Pride radiates from her smile, and she leans into his shoulder like he's her security blanket.

I know that feeling all too well. Even with Chad and others in the room, I've never felt safer in my life than I do when Rhett's near. It's definitely an odd feeling to have when you're in a jail, but somehow, I know he'd do anything to keep me safe, and it looks like Reba felt that way too.

I back out of the funeral home's website and return to my search.

The next three headlines are similar.

Police Search for Missing Fairhope Student.

Alabama State Police Requests Help from DNR to Find Missing Woman.

State Police Ending Search for Missing Woman.

It's the next one that hits me like a bucket of ice-cold water to the face.

Boone County Remains Identified as Missing Fairhope Woman.

I suck in a deep breath before clicking on the link.

"Human remains found in a local creek bed have been identified as Reba Darby, an 18-year-old Fairhope Community College student who vanished more than two months ago, state officials said.

Miguel Ramirez, a representative of the state coroner's office, said the remains: a partial human skull, femur, and several other bone fragments found by a mushroom hunter, exhibited signs that the victim's body

was burned prior to her remains ending up in the remote creek bed.

The state's investigation into her disappearance is still ongoing."

A lump burns in my throat.

She wasn't just murdered. Her body had been desecrated and thrown away like garbage. An act only a true monster could inflict on another human being. Yet the article didn't mention any arrests. All Rhett had told me was that her killer was in the jail.

Was her case still open?

Returning to the search page, I scroll down further until the title of an article rips away every ounce of air left in my lungs. ***"Man Charged with Murder of Fairhope Woman."*** My hand trembles over the mouse and it takes two tries to muster enough strength to click the button. The page loads slowly while my heart beats like a hummingbird inside my chest.

"Six months after identification of human remains, a suspect has been arrested in the murder of Reba Darby after a tip from the Crime Stoppers line led police to arrest an eighteen-year-old man."

The name on the next line freezes time and space.

"Chad Elscher, the ex-boyfriend of the victim, was formally charged this morning in Boone County Superior Court with the aggravated murder of Reba Darby. His arraignment date is pending."

My stomach boils, and through tear-filled eyes, I scramble from the bed and out into the yard. Bending forward, I heave and heave until there's nothing left of my dinner, leaving my head spinning in a dizzying haze.

Chad had killed Rhett's sister, and Rhett intends to kill Chad.

I have to stop him. But how?

STONEFACE

"HER DEATH WAS JUST *one terrible moment amongst so many wonderful ones."*

Delilah's voice floats through my head like a whisper. Over and over again, I've been hearing her say these words.

But she doesn't know the details. She doesn't know that Chad Elscher and his girlfriend had lured my sister to the house where she would meet her end. Delilah didn't know they brought her there to beat the shit out of her.

She didn't know that once they started beating her, they couldn't stop. They beat her until she was unconscious, and then they got scared. Scared of being caught for her murder, even though she wasn't fucking dead.

So they'd come up with a plan. They'd burned her body, but because she was still alive, she came to, screaming and struggling, trying to put out the flames engulfing her body, but it was Elscher who'd caved her head in with a baseball bat.

It was Elscher who had used that bat to break up her charred bones, gathered as much as he could up, and threw them in the river. It was Elscher who thought he'd gotten away with it, until his girlfriend couldn't take the guilt any longer and turned herself in.

Delilah didn't know that even though I was miles away on my first deployment, I felt Reba die—I felt a piece of *me* die. I'd felt the pain all over my body, though not nearly as intense as my sister did, and then I felt our connection snap.

When I'd made that phone call to the police to do a welfare check on Reba, they had thought I was nuts, dismissing my tethered twin connection as silliness. But Reba was missing, and it didn't take long for them to realize that our connection had been anything but silly. It had been our fucking lifeline.

How could I just let that shit go? How the fuck am I supposed to go on with my life knowing Elscher got out on parole? How am I supposed to stop punishing myself for not being there when Reba had needed me the most?

It had been our eighteenth birthday when I'd joined with the Marines. Momma had still been alive, though she was rarely home. Our momma had loved us, but she had also loved to gamble. When she wasn't working, she was at the casino, leaving us to spend most of our childhood on our own.

Reba had been the one who encouraged me to join.

"Go, Rhett. It's the only way either of us are gonna get out of this shit hole town. You go, see the world. I'll follow along behind you the first chance I get."

And I did. I'd made a quick trip home when Momma died, but even then, Reba had told me to go back. And when I'd deployed, she had sounded so excited on the phone.

"I'm so proud of you. Do you know that? I brag to all my friends that my brother is a tough guy Marine, off saving lives."

I remember chuckling at that. "I haven't saved a damn soul, ya nut job."

"But you will," she said. "But be safe, okay? Take care of you."

And that had been Reba in a nutshell. Upbeat. Positive. Always seeing the silver lining on every single gloomy looking rain cloud.

Delilah had been right about the way Reba would feel about my life choices. She was the only person I knew that could get a hit in on me without me expecting it. "Twin thing," she used to say, laughing at the stunned expression on my face.

She'd kick my ass if she knew what I was planning. She'd really kick it if she knew how I'd spent the past eighteen years, holding people at a distance, and not allowing myself to feel any other emotion other than anger.

"Her death was just one terrible moment amongst so many wonderful ones."

So many wonderful ones.

But how do I let that son of a bitch just walk away?

He's still an evil man who'll hurt someone else. He will abso-fucking-lutely re-offend. How do I just step back and let that happen?

Delilah's laughter rings in my ears, and I allow my thoughts to drift to the couple of kisses we'd shared. *Fuck me.* What is this woman doing to me?

I think about Judge and the rest of the Black Hoods. About the way they've stood by me, even though they don't know what the fuck is going on. About the ass kicking Judge will give me once I get out of here, simply for thinking I could walk away from them.

I think about Delilah and what it would be like to touch her whenever I wanted. To hold her and kiss her, and make love to her without being beaten to hell by a bunch of guards.

I even think about tiny Penny, and how nice it would be to have a home where she could curl up in my bed or sun herself on my front porch, living out the rest of her days being treated like the princess she is.

Is Chad Elscher really worth losing all of that?

Henry Tucker's terrified eyes flash to the forefront of my memories.

I'm no choir boy. I've killed before, more than once. And if anyone deserved to die, it was that motherfucker. But even so, being the one to deal him that fate feels like a black stain on my already fractured soul.

That stain will never wash away.

What kind of damage would killing Elscher do to what's left of my soul? And how do I just erase eighteen years of revenge plotting?

Like a slideshow on speed, the faces of Delilah, Penny, Judge, GP, and everyone else in my MC family play over and over in my mind.

If I end him, I lose them. I lost Reba to him already, and it's fucked up my entire life. If I lost my new family, what would the cost to me be this time?

"Guard," I call out, rushing over to the bars. "I need to call my lawyer."

DELILAH

AFTER PIECING TOGETHER everything about Chad and Rhett's sister, I have no other choice. The sheriff and I need to talk, whether he has time for me or not. I don't hesitate a single second before I push through the heavy doors near the back of the administration area. His secretary's eyes widen when she sees me.

"I need to speak with the sheriff," I demand of the blonde woman sitting behind the desk outside his office.

She looks me up and down from underneath her lashes, her judgment clear as day. "He's busy. I can leave him a message, if you'd like."

"I'm tired of leaving him messages."

Leaning over, I strain my neck and see him through his office window. His feet are propped up on his desk, a cup of coffee in his hand. "Doesn't look too busy to me." Sidestepping her desk, I make a beeline for his office.

Avoiding my emails and calls, he's left me with no other choice.

"You can't go in there," his secretary scolds, her high heels clicking like a typewriter as she chases after me. She reaches for my arm, but I shake her off and turn the knob, throwing open the door. The sheriff's eyes grow wide.

"What's the meaning of this?" he growls, his frown heavy as he slams his feet onto the floor and glares at his secretary, who skids to a stop behind me.

"I tried to stop her, Sheriff, but she just pushed her way in."

"It's fine, Dolores," he sighs, his words and expression full of fake sincerity. "Miss Walker must have something to say if she thinks she can just burst into my office without an appointment."

"Do you want me to stay, sir?" she asks sheepishly.

"No. Close the door on your way out." She does as he tells her, and the second the door clicks shut, he turns his authoritative stare to me. "You've got to either be the stupidest or bravest woman I've met to pull a stunt like that."

"You gave me no other choice."

"I'm a busy man, Miss Walker. I can't drop everything to help with a voluntary program when I have bigger fish to fry. It's an election year, you know, and I have to make my obligatory appearances." He's a jail sheriff, not some big shot like wardens at the state prisons.

He crosses his arms over his chest. "Well, you're here now, so out with it."

I don't allow his rudeness to deter me. "Chad Elscher. I want him out of my program."

Uncrossing his arms, he shifts his body and leans his elbows on his desk in front of him. "Dare I ask why you're issuing such a demand?"

I consider telling him everything. The connection between Rhett and Chad, and what I fear may happen, but that would only put a spotlight back on Rhett. He didn't deserve to be punished for something he didn't do… yet. And besides, this guy's an asshole. I don't want to tell him anything, other than I want this guy gone.

"Chad is a problem," I blurt out. "He has been since my prison program. I was working with the warden there to remove him before he transferred out."

"I'm going to need a little more information before I put a mark on someone's record that is up for parole."

Shit. Chad wasn't lying about the possibility of getting out. It's real. I can't let that happen, either. He'll only hurt someone else's family, and I can't let what happened to Reba happen to anyone else.

"Chad has an obsession with me, Sheriff. He finds ways to put himself near me, and it makes me uncomfortable."

"As men like him should. These men are thieves, drunkards, and in some cases, murderers. Being uncomfortable is to be expected, especially considering that you're a woman."

"My gender has nothing to do with the way he makes me feel," I fire back. "He's a danger to the entire program." Not only to me, but to Rhett as well.

"Miss Walker, I understand your plight, but I've received no other reports from any of our guards, even our female guards, that would corroborate on what you're saying. His records from the prison show he's a model citizen."

"A model citizen? He's a murderer—a killer. As for reports, the guard on duty had to order him to step away from me last week."

"If that really did occur, the guard didn't report it, nor did you. I can't make decisions if there's no report filed." His answer is so matter-of-fact, it takes me a second to recover from how nonchalantly he's taking my complaint. I'm not looking for attention, I'm looking for action. "Nothing you've told me gives me any cause to agree to what you're asking, Miss Walker."

"I've been trying to report it for weeks. You just didn't make yourself available to me."

"You didn't try hard enough."

I have plenty of evidence to the contrary, but

revealing it means putting Rhett in the crosshairs. Could I do that to him?

He's just as dangerous as anyone else here, but there's something about him. A piece of him locked away inside himself. I'm not even sure he knew it was there until now. Seeing him with Penelope was the start of it. His gentleness with her and understanding, despite his smart-ass comments.

He loves her, just as he loved his sister.

Someone who has that much capacity to love deserves to get his second chance, even if that path leads him away from me. He deserves it. I can't put him in that position. You don't intentionally hurt someone you love.

Love. *I love him.* The realization hits me like a ton of bricks. This isn't just about me anymore, it's about him, about us. That's what brought me here today. Not protecting myself or getting Chad out of this program, but protecting him from repeating history. To protect him from himself doing the only thing I know to do, which is putting myself on the line to find some way to prevent it.

"If you're not going to remove him, then give me extra guards. It'll make me feel safer knowing I have extra eyes in the room."

"My jail is safe, Miss Walker."

"Safe? An inmate was killed here recently in a yard fight. That's not what I would call 'safe.'"

"And how would you know about that?" he inquires,

arching his brow. "That information is not public knowledge."

"I just know, okay? Chad's been given the opportunity to get close to me on a number of occasions because the guard assigned to the kennel would rather play on his phone than do his job. I want him out. Today."

"The answer is no," he answers flatly.

"To which request?"

"Both of them."

"So it's fine with you that I'm at risk, but not those who signed up for this line of work?" *Keep trying. There has to be some kind of leeway. Common ground to make sure Rhett is never alone, or has the opportunity to do what he thinks he wants to do to Chad. He can't have that. It'll ruin everything.*

"Did you not yourself sign up for this program, Miss Walker?"

"I did, but—"

"Does this jail and the taxpayers who support it not pay you for your services?"

"They do," I admit.

"Being close to inmates should be a given."

A given? Oh, hell no. He's not going to victim blame me for putting myself into this situation when it's his own guards who are too lax.

"Until you bring me credible evidence that Chad

Elscher is a danger to you or those in the program, he stays with no extra guards."

"So that's it, then? You're giving me an impossible choice. Pull my program and lose the funding that helps keep my rescue running, or put my life in danger because you won't take how that man makes me feel into consideration because you have no documented evidence from your guards. I'll be sure to remember that when something does happen."

"It seems that I am." He shifts in his seat and reaches for a pen. "Though I do have one remaining question for you." He sits straighter in his chair with a smug expression on his face. Bringing his hands up, he laces his fingers together. "I've been given reports of special permissions being granted to you to work one-on-one with an inmate. A Mr. Rhett Darby, from my understanding. It seems to me that one-on-one work isn't an opposition to you as long as it's with certain persons, so why does Mr. Elscher pose a threat to you when you're willingly putting yourself into that position by your own request?"

My heart stops. He knows about us. Oh, God. How is that possible? No one should know. I didn't even know until today how I felt about him. Not until I decided that protecting his future meant more than having one of my own.

"Unlike the other animals, Mr. Darby's needs special

care," I answer with a half-truth. "A part of my job is teaching the care of animals as a method for rehabilitation and therapy. It's the entire point of my program."

"And who are you rehabilitating exactly? The dog or the man?"

Rage boils under the surface the more he throws out veiled accusations of my involvement with Rhett. Should I have assigned Penelope to this program in normal cases? No, but the way she's bonded with him tells me I made the right choice, despite everything else. Did I mean to fall for him? Absolutely not, but it happened, and I don't regret it at all. Yet the sheriff knowing about it is a major problem. He's going to make trouble for me no matter what answer I give him, and he knows it.

"If that will be all, Miss Walker, I do have more pressing matters to attend to today."

"I won't forget this," I warn, my disappointment and anger seething inside of me. Coming to him was a mistake. Men like him, they don't understand what it is to be uncomfortable or scared around another human being who has more power than you do. He's never been made to feel marginalized or dismissed.

Power corrupts even those with good intentions, after all, and it's innocent people who pay the price for their self-serving decisions.

I guess it's up to me to make sure it doesn't happen, but how am I going to do that?

STONEFACE

I WALK into the small room set aside for inmates to meet with their legal counsel, and can't help but gape at the tiny woman sitting beside Judge.

She's petite, blonde, beautiful, and extremely young. Add to that her pink pencil skirt and blazer, you have yourself the least likely biker lawyer in all the free world.

But considering Judge is perched on the chair beside her, I know this is no mistake.

Standing as I approach the table, she waits for the guards to adjust the handcuffs. "It's nice to finally meet you, Mr. Darby. My name is Brooke Miller-Stewart. I'm a partner at Miller, Stewart, & Cline Law Office here in Austin, and I have been hired by our mutual friend here to be your legal counsel."

I look at Judge and smirk. "Since when does the club have Barbie covering our legal issues?"

Judge chuckles, but doesn't answer. Brooke Miller-Stewart does, though.

"First of all, Mr. Darby, my name is not Barbie, it's Brooke. I may be blonde, but I am no bimbo. You will treat me with the respect all women deserve, and you will keep your sexist opinions to yourself. We clear?"

Judge's grin grows wider as mine disappears. "Yes, ma'am."

Brooke nods and takes a seat, pulling the stack of papers in front of her a little closer and picking up a pen. "My secretary informs me that you would like to cooperate now."

I nod. "I want out."

She arches her brow. "You could've been out of here a long time ago, Mr. Darby, but you kept refusing to see me."

"You and everyone else," Judge mutters, leaning back in his chair.

I ignore him. "Well, I'm cooperating now, and I want out of here."

Brooke presses her lips together, considering that. "This isn't a state-run hotel, Mr. Darby. You are here because you stole a police car and evaded arrest."

Judge snorts. "If by evading arrest, you mean driving like a little old woman that lost her glasses, then sure, he evaded arrest. But he did it at a ridiculously slow speed."

Brooke doesn't even crack a smile. "Regardless,

you're facing a third-degree felony grand theft auto charge, as well as driving under the influence and resisting arrest. All of those charges are serious on their own, but the three of them together could earn you some serious time."

To Judge, I say, "Isn't she full of good fucking news?"

Brooke's lips twitch just a little bit at that. "If you plead guilty, you're looking at two to ten years in the state prison, including time served, as well as a fine of up to ten thousand dollars."

"Jesus," Judge mutters.

"And if I fight it?"

Brooke places her pen on the table. "Well, you can't exactly plead not guilty. They have you on surveillance footage from the convenience store, walking out with your case of beer and climbing inside the cruiser."

Judge shakes his head slowly, burying his face in his hands.

"And every cop in the city was following you that night, meaning every dashcam available was trained on you. And that wouldn't have been so bad if you had just been in the driver's seat, but you were definitely not. I've seen the footage. You were leaning out the window for a good portion of the 'chase,' at which point you were flipping off the pursuing officers and screaming profanities at them."

"Such a fucking jackass," Judge barks.

"It seemed like a good idea at the time," I joke, but Judge isn't in a laughing mood.

He sits a little straighter and turns to face her. "So what're our options?"

"One, we do nothing, take our chances in court, and likely end up in jail for years and pay whatever the judge deems an appropriate fine. But, considering you're a biker, and you took a police vehicle for your little joy ride, I doubt the judge would be feeling particularly forgiving toward you."

"Next," Judge says, his face back in his hands.

"We take a plea deal. The prosecution is offering a deal for five years, less time served, plus five years' probation."

Five fucking years.

If you would've told me I'd get five years just a few days ago, I'd have told you I couldn't care less. But that was before I realized I still had shit to offer. Before I realized I wanted to be with Delilah outside of these prison walls. Before I came to the very powerful understanding that I am letting my sister down by being in this jail right now.

"Please tell me there's a third option."

Brooke leans forward. "We use your military credentials. I looked you up. You were a sniper for the Marines, correct?"

My jaw tightens, but I nod.

"We explain what you've done for our country. We explain that you lost your entire team to an improvised explosive device, and that you were the only survivor. We tell them about your PTSD as a result, and the fact that you quit taking your meds a couple of months before the incident took place."

"Jesus Christ, woman. How do you know all this shit about me?"

"I wouldn't be much of a lawyer if I didn't look a little deeper into my clients, now would I?"

Judge frowns. "Even I didn't know most of this shit."

"You can take that up with my client after I'm gone."

Fuck. I haven't told the club about Reba, or about losing my team. Most of them knew I was a sniper, but that's as much as I'd ever shared. Making this plea would bring all that messy shit from my past out into the light for everyone to see.

Delilah's sweet smile flashes in my mind, and I don't have to give it another thought. "Let's use it. Tell it all if you think it'll get me off."

"Why did you do that shit anyway?" Judge finally asks. "That's the part I never understood."

"It's a long fucking story, Judge. I promise you, once I'm out of here, I'll share every last detail with you, but not today."

Judge doesn't seem satisfied with that, but he tips his head, telling me he'll let it go, for now.

And then I remember. "That little gift you arranged for me came in very handy the other day," I say, holding his gaze.

At first, he looks confused, but once he realizes I'm talking about the shiv and Henry Tucker, his eyes fill with relief.

And then, even though he's not supposed to touch me, he reaches across the table and puts his heavy hand on mine. "Thank you doesn't even cut it, brother. You've released so many in our family from a world of hurt."

It's not until that moment I realize the Black Hoods had done the same for me all along. They'd unknowingly taken my hurt and absorbed it into their brotherhood. Without them, I'd have fallen to pieces long ago.

"You've done that for me too," I tell him, and I know he understands.

DELILAH

I NEED to tell Rhett what I've learned. That I know all about his sister's murder, and that Chad was the one who had killed her. The thought of keeping my knowledge a secret from him has burned a hole in my stomach, making me toss and turn over the last few nights.

He needs to know. Part of me is terrified that he won't exactly appreciate my internet sleuthing, but another part—a very important part—knows I have to bring him around. He can't do what he came here to do. No matter how brutal his sister's murder was, Rhett doesn't belong here. He belongs on the outside, with or without me.

I also need to tell him about the sheriff, and that he knows about my one-on-one time with him.

I stomp through the entrance of the jail and head straight for the kennels, not stopping to talk to anyone. I pass a few guards as I turn down the hallway, and one of them makes a point of winking at me. *Weird.*

I shove the uneasiness aside and continue on my way. I need to stay laser focused before I lose my nerve about talking to Rhett.

I'm nearly at the heavy metal door that leads into the kennel when a hand clamps onto my arm. Quickly tugging me through a door I hadn't even noticed before, I go to scream, but a hand clamps down over my mouth, and my back lands against something hard. A door slams behind me, plunging me and my attacker into total darkness. It all happens so fast.

With every ounce of strength I can muster, I fight. I squirm and kick, and shriek out a nearly inaudible scream muffled by someone's meaty palm.

"Jesus, woman," a voice whispers in my ear. "Take it easy." Whoever has me shifts his body and mine, and suddenly a bare lightbulb clicks on overhead.

"You asshole!" I whisper-shout, nearly in tears. "You scared the shit out of me."

Rhett stands before me, a smug grin on his face.

I smack his arm. "What do you think you're doing? Do you want to get an extra charge added?"

Chuckling, he wraps his arms around my waist, tugging me closer. "For what? Kidnapping? It's a closet."

I take in the small room. We are indeed inside a closet.

"Someone's going to notice," I hiss.

"No, they won't." Burying his nose in my neck, his lips brush against the sensitive skin just below my ear. "The guard is a friend of sorts. We've got fifteen minutes."

His lips press tender kisses all along my throat, his arm around my waist pulling me closer, bending me backward, forcing me to submit to the delicious way his body feels against mine.

"I need to tell you something," I say, barely able to breathe.

"It can wait," he replies, his mouth moving to cover mine. I shove him away, and he leans back, his gaze holding mine. "We don't have much time, Flower Child. This may be our only shot."

His eyes are filled with the same need I've been battling for weeks now, and suddenly, I don't want to think about murder or revenge, or that sick bastard, Chad. I want to wrap myself up in this beautiful man and make him feel as good as he makes me feel with just a look.

"Fuck it." Reaching out, I grab the sides of his face and pull him to me, crushing my lips to his.

Rhett leans into me, his hands at my pants, tugging on the button of my jeans. As soon as they pop open, he tears his lips from mine and kneels before me, dragging my pants and panties down with him.

My cheeks flame as he buries his nose between my legs and inhales.

"You smell so fucking good, Flower Child," he growls. His tongue comes out and slides along the crease. He can't reach much in this position, but when the tip of his tongue drags across my clit, my knees nearly buckle.

"God," I pant.

Pressing his nose into my mound, he flicks it again and again, sucking and nipping at it, pulling that tiny bundle of nerves to the point where I can barely breathe.

"Quiet, baby." His voice vibrates against me. "If we get caught, we're both in the shit."

Clapping a hand over my mouth, I place my other hand on the back of his silky-smooth head. In rhythm with his tongue, I roll my hips, giving his tongue more access to my sweet spot by pressing his face tighter to my body.

My release hits me like a tidal wave, washing me out to a sea of utter euphoria, and I happily ride it, moaning and panting into my hand.

"Fuck, baby." Getting to his feet, he reaches for his pants and spins me around. "Hands on the wall," he orders.

I hear the crinkle of a condom wrapper as I place my hands on the wall in front of me. Spreading my legs apart, as far as they'll go with my jeans still wrapped around my ankles, he presses his hand on my back, bending me forward until my bare ass hits the heat radiating off his very hard, very large erection.

"Oh, God," I gasp.

Rhett enters me in one swift, quick motion, filling me entirely, barely pausing as his hips begin their steady, delicious rhythm.

"Pussy feels so fucking good," he groans, grasping my hips in his hands and slamming my ass back onto him. "Fucking perfect."

Me, I can't say a word. I can't breathe. I can't talk. All I can do is try to keep my moans to a minimum and enjoy the thorough pleasure I'm feeling at this moment.

A second release coils itself low in my belly, and this time, every part of me feels like it's on fire.

"Fuck," I gasp. "Harder, Rhett."

Skin slaps against skin, and I have to adjust my hands to prevent my head from slamming into the wall. But I don't fucking care, because this time, Rhett rides the wave with me.

My orgasm shatters every ounce of tension in my body, and all I can feel is him. Me, him, and perfection, as he shivers with his own release.

We stay that way for a moment, both of us panting. I don't know about him, but I'm smiling from ear to ear.

"Rhett," I whisper, slowly bringing myself to a standing position and reaching for my pants.

A rap at the door has me nearly leaping out of my own damn skin. "Time to go, big guy," a voice calls from the other side. "Wrap it up."

Rhett tucks himself back into his pants, condom and all, and smiles down at me. Pressing his lips to my forehead, he holds me close. "You're an amazing woman, Flower Child. And this right here,"—he motions around the tiny closet—"I won't forget this. Not ever."

He turns, then, putting himself closer to the door and shielding me from being seen. "Don't go," I plead. "We need to talk."

"We will, baby, but I have to go."

He plants one last kiss on my lips, and then he's gone.

STONEFACE

"HE'S A DANGER TO SOCIETY." My old buddy Dolan is on the witness stand, explaining his version of what had gone on the night I'd stolen his cruiser.

"It states on your report that he was driving twenty-five miles per hour. Is that not an accurate number?" Brooke Miller-Stewart doesn't fuck around. She's managed to turn every word out of Dolan's mouth right back on him, making him look like a fool.

"It's accurate," he replies, his jaw tight.

"So, I'm confused, Officer Dolan. If he was simply driving at such a slow rate of speed, he wasn't exactly endangering any lives, or am I missing something here?"

"He had every officer in the precinct following him."

Brooke nods. "At any point, did the chase become violent?"

Dolan sighs. "No, but—"

"At any point, was your life in danger?"

"No, but—"

"Did my client hit anyone with your police cruiser?"

Dolan's face darkens to a deep shade of red. "He didn't, but—"

"Did my client fight back when you arrested him?"

"No, but—"

"So, then, how exactly can you make the statement that Mr. Darby here is a danger to society when at no point was any part of society actually in danger?"

"He stole my fucking cruiser," Dolan snaps. "If that's not a danger to society, I don't know what is."

Brooke leans her ass against the defendant's table and tents her fingers near her lips, as if considering his words. "It also states in your report that Mr. Darby resisted arrest. Is that a correct statement?"

Dolan sits up a little straighter. "Yes, it is."

"But I've reviewed that dash cam footage, Mr. Dolan, and when Mr. Darby exits the cruiser in question, he does so with his hands up, drops to his knees, and submits to the arrest. So what part of that did you consider resisting arrest?"

"He wouldn't pull over!" Dolan cries, then locks eyes with the prosecutor, who looks like he'd rather be just about anywhere than here. "What's going on? Why aren't you objecting?"

Low voices and surprised gasps come from all over

the courtroom, and Brooke turns to give me a reassuring wink.

"Order," Judge Henderson calls, slamming his gavel down on the bench once, twice, three times. "Officer Dolan, I will remind you that you are in a court of law. You're on a witness stand to answer questions, not ask them. Are we clear?"

Properly chastised, Dolan settles back into the witness seat. "We're clear."

The judge glares at him for a moment more, and then motions to Brooke. "Continue."

"Officer Dolan, during booking, Mr. Darby wound up with a severely broken nose. Can you describe to me how that happened?"

Dolan freezes.

Brooke allows him to sweat without saying a word for an uncomfortably long amount of time before she continues. "You'll be happy to know that you don't have to explain that to the court today, Officer, because I've actually pulled the footage from the booking area of the jail, and have it all on video."

"Objection," the prosecutor challenges. "Officer Dolan is not the one on trial here."

"Overruled," Judge Henderson says, leaning toward the witness stand. "How did Mr. Darby come by that broken nose?"

Dolan sighs. "He stole my fucking cruiser, and then

he was mocking me. I was pissed off and got a little carried away."

"So you used unnecessary force while booking my client? Is that what you're saying?"

Dolan glowers. "Yes."

"So maybe it's you who's a danger to society for being unable to rein in your temper, don't you think, Officer Dolan?"

The prosecutor jumps to his feet. "Objection!"

Brooke throws her hands up in the air. "Withdrawn. But let the record show that Officer Dolan himself broke a few laws here as well, so his opinion on the safety of society when it comes to Rhett Darby is most definitely biased."

Judge Henderson shakes his head. After ascertaining that Brooke is finished with her cross-examination, he leans forward.

"It's clear to me that there's more to this case than meets the eye. Mr. Darby. Your service to our country will be taken into consideration, as will Officer Dolan's mistreatment of the entire situation. Let's set a date for one weeks' time to meet back here and discuss possible ruling and sentencing."

With a bang of the gavel, my case is dismissed until next week, and I'm led from the courtroom. As I'm about to step out the door, I can't help but smirk at Officer Dolan as he glares daggers in my direction.

DELILAH

THE FAMILIAR, ear-piercing repetition of dogs barking inside of their kennels echoes off the high ceilings as the last member of today's class slips out the door. I nod at the guard that had stayed back to wait for me as I step into the enclosed kennel section of the room to do one last check on the animals.

Today's class had been surprisingly good, considering Rhett had been away for his court date. Mostly because he wasn't the only inmate missing. Chad hadn't been here today, either. Did the sheriff have second thoughts after our rather heated conversation?

A girl could dream.

"Good night, sweet pea," I call into Penelope's kennel and smile when she yips out a goodbye of her own. My smile grows when I recall the folded note I'd found in her collar this morning.

Don't go finding some other criminal to fall for. I'll be back tomorrow.

My heart feels a little lighter, knowing he was thinking of me, and had found a way to communicate, despite not being here in person. He did care about me, even if he didn't say it aloud.

Not that we had the chance to really talk. I haven't laid eyes on him since our very hot and steamy closet rendezvous. That conversation I'd been desperate to have with him is still lingering.

On the bright side, though, him being away from the jail means there's distance between him and Chad. Distance between Chad and me had been an added bonus.

I toss a few loose toys into the toy bin and check the supply levels in the storage room. Everything looks good and ready to go for tomorrow.

"I'm going to just check the dog run outside," I call to the guard as I pass.

He pushes off the wall and follows behind me toward the outer doors. He calls over the radio to the control room, and the door buzzes open. Reaching for it, he allows me to go ahead of him before stepping out behind me.

"I won't be long. Just checking the progress on the new fence." He nods and stays near the door as I walk out into the sunny yard.

With the state of the old fence, Ashley had closed down this section until work could be done. The sheriff, of course, was against spending any money on it, so we had raised the funds to pay for it ourselves. It took a little longer than we had hoped, but with a large donation to the program, we were able to fully fund the repair, as well as buy extra outdoor kennels with sunshades. The kennels had already been constructed, and the fence was almost done. I hated that these poor dogs had been cooped up inside for the last several months, but that will be ending soon.

After ensuring that all is coming along nicely, I turn around and head back toward the door where the guard was waiting. When an arm wraps around my chest, tugging me into a dark corner of the construction area, I panic at first, but then smile, remembering how wonderful our last secret encounter had been, so I lean into the embrace.

"Court didn't take long," I whisper, spinning around. My blood turns to ice when I realize this is definitely not Rhett, but Chad.

"My hearing is still a few days away, sweet cheeks," Chad says, his hot, rancid breath hitting my face. My stomach churns. Where's the guard? How did Chad even get out here? *Oh, God. We're alone.*

"Chad," I say, trying to keep the trembling out of my voice. "What are you doing here?"

"I came to see you. I figured you might miss me after the sheriff had me removed from the program, and from Missy."

Fuck.

"You shouldn't be out here." Frantic, I look around the outdoor kennels. No guards. No other inmates. We're truly and utterly alone.

"Looking for the guard?" Chad sneers. "Got a friend dealing with him, so he's a little busy at the moment."

No, no, no. This can't be happening.

I have to get to that door and hit the button to get back inside. That's the only way I get out of here. *Think, Delilah, think. How do I get away from him without him catching me?* I could try to run for it, but I'd never make it.

Fighting my way out is also off the table. Chad has at least four inches and sixty pounds on me. He could overpower me without even trying. That leaves me with only one option until I can think of a better idea. Get him talking, and pray someone comes along and catches him before he hurts me, or worse.

"Fear looks good on you, Delilah." His lips graze my neck and I shudder. Rhett had showered kisses on that same spot just a few days ago, and I had felt nothing but heat and desire. Chad's lips make me want to curl up inside myself and disappear into darkness.

"You need to let me go, Chad." A single tear escapes

and races down my cheek. It's quickly followed by another, and another.

"Why?" he breathes, his arm around my chest moving as he slides his hand across me, cupping my breast.

"Your parole hearing," I whisper. God, I can't breathe. "You're getting out, remember? You're going to be free. If you get caught with me, they'll never let you out."

"Nobody's going to catch us." His confidence in that statement sends my heart plummeting to my feet. "My cellie has the guard. I'd be surprised if that prick is still alive at this point."

Suddenly, he spins me around and grasps my wrists, pressing me against the chain-link fence. "Why don't you just admit it, Delilah? You think you're better than me. I've spent all this time trying to get your attention, and you think I'm some worthless piece of shit."

Goose bumps break out along my scalp. I know if he wasn't holding me up, my knees would give out completely. "No, Chad. That's not true at all."

"Bullshit," he spits, shoving me harder into the fence, his nose just inches from mine. "That's fucking bullshit, and you know it. That's why you had the sheriff take me out of this program. That's why you turned me down when I asked you for a date. You're a snotty little bitch who probably has her pussy sewed shut just to torture men like me."

He pulls me forward and slams me back again, causing the fence to jingle and quake.

"But you're not better than me, Delilah. You need to learn you can't come in here and get us guys all worked up, then leave us with absolutely nothing. You're a cock tease. A stupid, dirty fucking cock tease."

His eyes drag up and down my body, and my heart lurches. With just that one look, I can tell he's done talking.

"Chad, please."

"Chad, please," he mocks, his voice high and screechy.

I try to move, but there's nowhere to go. He has me backed up against the fence, and his body dwarfs mine. But his hands are on my wrists, which means…

With a roar of frustration and exertion, I bring up my knee and slam it into his groin. Or, at least, I try to. Anticipating my move, Chad brings up his leg and shields his front.

Pissed off now, I kick, scream, bite, and flail, doing everything I can think of to wrench myself away from him, until finally, he's had enough.

He spins me around, shoving his hand into the back of my head, cramming it against the fence, his other hand coming down to fumble with my belt.

Still screaming at the top of my lungs, I continue to fight. I almost get away too, but Chad's fingers tangle into my hair, and he's on the move, dragging me behind him like a dog on a leash, all the way to a closed off supply shed next to the kennels.

He wrenches the door open and throws me inside. I dig my heels in, trying to stop him. or at least slow him down, but it's useless. I crash against the far wall and Chad steps inside, closing the door behind him.

"Cozy. Not even that big bastard you like so much can stop me now."

"He'll be mad if something happens to me," I blurt out, shoving my back up against the wall until I'm almost standing.

Chad's brow furrows. "Who fucking cares? You think I care about that motherfucker?"

Chad grips me by the elbow and jerks me back to him. My face is only inches from his. "You're fucking him, aren't you?"

With every last ounce of breath I have left inside of me, I hold his stare and scream out as loud as I can, "Fuck. You!"

Chad's fist slams into my cheek, and I would swear it almost came out the other side. Stumbling back, I clutch my face and scream again. "Somebody, help me!"

This time, he grabs me by the throat and shoves me down on the ground. His fingers squeeze, and I can't catch a breath as he climbs on top of me. All I can do is plead up at him with my eyes.

And this is how I'm going to die.

He leans over me, his forehead pressing mine into the concrete floor. "Answer me! Are you fucking him?" Reaching down between us, he forces his hand beneath the waistband of my jeans and directly between my legs, groping me with his thick, stubby fingers. "Has he touched you here?"

"Yes," I snarl through gritted teeth.

His open palm splits my lips, and I can taste the blood as it runs from my nose.

I can't hold my tears any longer. "Please," I sob. "Just let me go."

His wicked grin tells me he's getting off on this. My fear turns him on.

His erection grows against my leg and he thrusts it against me. "You feel that, baby? That's for you."

Grunting with the effort, I struggle against his grip, lifting my hips and kicking, doing anything I can to knock him off of me.

"That a girl," he coaxes. "Keep fighting."

His mouth covers mine as he grinds against me, and the position I'm in, lying on my back, prevents me from jerking away. So instead, I suck his lip in deeper and bite down as hard as I can.

The metallic taste of his blood floods into my mouth as he hisses in pain. He tries to pull away, but I have his lip locked tight between my teeth.

He rears back and punches me in the stomach once, twice, three times, before I finally release him.

"Stupid fucking bitch!" he roars. His hands come up and again wrap around my throat. I can't breathe. I can't talk. I have no doubt I'm going to die for real this time.

Closing my eyes, I prepare myself for what's coming when I finally slip away.

But then he's gone. My head throbs as I struggle to breathe from the lingering pressure around my throat. The room spins as I force myself up into a sitting position.

That's when I see Chad on his knees before me, his eyes wide and bulging out, his face blue. Behind him is Buddy, who's screaming words I can't make out. And around Chad's throat is Rocco's leash.

Chad claws at it, desperate to get a taste of oxygen, but Buddy pulls it tighter. "Don't hurt women." He yanks the leash again, and then we hear a sickening *crunch*.

Chad's lifeless body slumps to the ground in front of me. Buddy remains motionless, staring at the leash in his hands before he tosses it onto the ground next to Chad, slides down onto his knees, and cries.

"I promised Mama I wouldn't hurt nobody again," he sobs. "She told me to be a good boy, and to keep my hands to myself.

"It's okay," I whisper, crawling a little closer to my giant savior, my voice painfully raw.

"No, it's not." He rubs his hands against both sides of his head. "Stepdaddy was mean to my momma. I tried to save her, and I killed him. Mama told me not to do it again before she died." He goes silent for a moment before breaking into sobs again. "I broke my promise."

"You saved my life," I rasp.

"Mama's gonna be so mad." I scoot closer to hug him, but a crowd of guards come rushing in, flooding the outdoor kennel. One of them grabs me by the arm, dragging me out of the space, while the others surround Buddy and Chad. Buddy yells when they throw him to the ground. A guard jams his knee into his back, keeping him down. They wrestle cuffs onto him and force him upright. Buddy shakes with fear when they walk past me.

"No," I try to yell, only for it to come out as a forced whisper. The exertion makes my head pound harder. *They can't do this. He saved me.* They drag him away from the scene, and he watches me until they take him around the corner, out of sight.

My pleas fall on deaf ears before the world spins and turns dark around me.

STONEFACE

RIDING HIGH from my court case earlier, I arrive back in the cell block just in time for supper. I grab my tray and glare down at the gruel on it, thanking my lucky stars I had a badass Barbie like Brooke working to get my ass out of here and off to where people keep the real food.

I plop down in my usual spot and scan the crowd for Buddy. He's always here first, so the fact that I beat him means I'm on a roll today.

"Hey, man." Gibbs plops down at the table, taking his time arranging his tray before looking directly at me. "Look, uh… some shit went down while you were gone, and I'm gonna tell you, but…" He glances around. "You gotta promise to keep your shit together, okay?"

My fists clench as I stare at him, not liking where this is going. "What is it?"

Gibbs sighs. "You gotta promise, man."

I lean closer. "Gibbs, no disrespect, but if you want to keep your head exactly where it is on your shoulders, you'll fucking tell me what's going on."

Gibbs swallows and takes a moment to collect himself. "Okay. So, Buddy's gone."

"What do you mean, gone? How can Buddy just be gone?"

"Something happened earlier, and they cleared out his cell. I think he's in solitary, but only until they're able to move him to the state prison. Pretty sure he's not coming back here."

A heavy ball of dread forms deep in my gut. "Explain."

Gibbs raises his hands. "Now, I just know what I heard, okay? I don't know the details, but from what I was told by one of the guys in solitary until a couple of hours ago, some shit went down in the animal rescue program. I heard a lady was attacked."

My body goes rigid.

Gibbs continues. "Now, I don't know if it was your lady or a guard or what. All I know is that a woman was attacked by an inmate, and Buddy walked in on it. Pretty sure he killed the guy."

"And what happened to the woman?"

Gibbs presses his lips together and shakes his head. "I

don't know. I heard there was an ambulance here, though."

"Jesus." I jump out of my seat and rush toward the bubble where two guards sit watching us. "Where's Buddy?" I ask, unable to stand still, my whole body vibrating.

"I can't tell you that," the guard says, a sad look in his eyes.

"What happened? Who was the lady that was attacked? Is she okay?"

The guard stands and moves a little closer. "Look, I can't give you any information on this at all. It's still under investigation, and I honestly don't know the specifics of it, anyway. All I can tell you is that Buddy is okay, but he won't be coming back to this cell block."

"What about the lady? Can you at least tell me who it was?

The guard looks around as if ensuring nobody else can hear us. "You didn't hear it from me, Darby, but I don't think your animal program will be continuing after this."

Holy fuck. What the fuck is that supposed to mean?

I move toward the door. "I need to go to the kennels. I need someone to take me down there."

"I'm sorry, Darby, but that's not going to be possible."

I run a hand along the top of my head and draw in a

breath, trying to maintain some semblance of control. "I need to see her."

The guard doesn't say another word, but the apology in his eyes does very little to ease my mind. How the fuck am I supposed to find out what's happening when I'm behind these fucking bars?

The guards will never tell me, and I can't just walk out and go see for myself.

"Fuck!" I roar, making a beeline for the row of telephones attached to the wall on the far side of the room.

Picking up the closest one, I press the buttons necessary to call Judge.

"Miss me already?" he says, a smile in his voice as he greets me.

"Judge…" I clutch the receiver so hard, I'm surprised it doesn't burst into dust. "I need a favor."

"Name it." The smile is gone from his voice, and now he's all business.

"I need you to find my girl. I need you to make sure she's okay."

Judge says nothing for a long time. And then, after I begin to wonder if he's still on the line, he barks out, "Since when do you have a fucking girl."

DELILAH

BEEPS AND MURMURING break the silence in my ears as the darkness finally lifts. My eyelids feel as if they weigh ten thousand pounds as I try to open them. It takes a few tries, but finally, I pry them apart, but everything is blurry.

With a great amount of effort, I lift my trembling hand up to my face and wince in pain as my fingertips graze along my swollen cheeks. And then I touch upon the thick padding of a collar around my neck.

Did he break my neck?

Oh, God. Chad—he'd done this. And Buddy. Poor, poor Buddy. What had happened to him?

My chest heaves, and the entire world spins around me as I try to push myself up into a sitting position. Alarms blare from behind me, and two people come running into my room.

"Breathe in as slowly, deeply, and gently as you can through your nose," a nurse to my left instructs me. Taking my hand, she holds my gaze as she breathes along with me.

"What's…happening?" I force out between labored breaths.

"Push another 2 milligrams of diazepam," a man in a white coat orders from the other side of me.

The nurse releases my hand and rushes out of the room.

"Miss Walker, I'm Dr. Fulbright. Do you know where you are?"

"No." God, my throat hurts so bad. "What's… happening… to me?"

"The ambulance brought you to St. David's." He presses his fingers against my wrist. "You're having a panic attack. I need you to do what the nurse showed you. In and out. Focus on your breathing."

I try to do what they want me to do, but it hurts so much. I feel as if I'm sucking in air that's going nowhere. The nurse returns and pushes a needle into an IV bag hanging on a stand next to me.

"You may feel a little dizzy when the medication takes effect."

It takes only a few seconds before a warm feeling washes over me. My body feels light after a few minutes, like I could fly away if I weren't lying on the bed, but my breathing slows back down. The doctor monitors my vitals and my breathing until the beeping stops.

"Do you know what happened?"

"Attacked."

"That's right. You're going to see a bright light, but I need you to keep your eyes open." Pulling a penlight from his pocket, he shines it into my eyes. Easier said than done for me, with the marching band practicing in my head. I flinch, recoiling in pain.

"Reflexes look normal," he mutters to himself. "We're going to run some tests to make sure you haven't sustained fractures on your neck. Let's do a chest X-ray, head CT, and a full blood workup. I'll be back to check on you shortly."

He disappears through the open door, and the nurse types away at the computer next to me. I close my eyes, focusing on my breathing, and send up a prayer to the big guy in the sky, thanking him for making it possible to still be here.

"Water?"

She hands me a paper cup from the tray and helps me maneuver it over the collar around my neck. The cool liquid feels so good as I drink it down.

When I finish, I hand her back the cup. "Thank you."

"I'll be right back, Miss Walker." Pulling up an attached remote on the bed next to me, she shows me the emergency call button. "If you need anything, or start having issues with your breathing, I want you to hit this button right here." She turns to leave, and for the first time, I'm alone with only the sounds of the machines and the normal white noise of an emergency room.

Closing my eyes, I concentrate on my breathing. In. Out. In. Out.

Loud, heavy footsteps approach the door.

"Sir, you can't go in there," a feminine voice scolds from the other side.

"I'm family." A man steps into the room, his large frame filling the doorway. He's an older man with a graying beard, but I don't recognize him. My hand slips down to the emergency call button when he takes three long strides and stops at my bedside.

"StoneFace sent me. Couldn't come himself, but asked me to check on you."

"Who are you?"

"Judge. His club president and friend."

"Club?"

He wipes his large hand across his face. "He's a member of my motorcycle club." He points to a black and white patch on his shoulder with the word "President" in bold, heavy script on the leather vest he's wearing. The man takes note of my confusion. "Didn't he tell you?"

I shake my head.

"Figures that big bastard didn't mention it. Guess

you two have some things to talk about when he gets out."

"Gets out?" Has something changed? I thought it was just a hearing.

"Only a matter of time." He looks at me before smiling. "You must be something special for him to ask me to check on you. Didn't even know he had a girl until he called. All I knew is he asked for you to be a character witness for his case."

He called me *his girl*. While a part of me melts at hearing someone say that out loud, we hadn't really made anything official yet. But clearly, he had done that on my behalf.

"I need you to tell me everything that happened, darling. Your man is going crazy in that jail."

I hesitate to open up to a stranger. I don't know this guy from Adam, but Rhett wouldn't have sent me someone he didn't trust.

"I get it. You don't have a fucking clue who I am. I wouldn't want to talk to me, either, but Rhett wanted me to pass along a message. Something about bows, and Flower Child." Cocking his brow, he gives me a cheeky smirk. "Y'all into some weird shit?"

I crack my first smile. I start to answer, swallowing to moisten my throat again. "No. He calls me Flower Child. The bows are about Penelope." Everything comes out like a whisper, but it hurts less this time.

"The fuck is that?"

"His dog."

"He got a dog? Shit, he and I apparently need to talk too." He lets out a belly laugh. "Knew the guy was weird, but if the last couple weeks have taught me anything, it's that the big guy has some layers. Who goes to jail and gets a pet?"

I giggle, but damn, if it hurts. I pull my hands up to my chest, trying to soften the blow.

"I was attacked, in the outside kennels," I start. "I don't know what happened to the guard, but one of the inmates got me alone. He was going to…" I take a moment to get my bearings. "I tried to fight back, but I couldn't."

Judge reaches out his big hand and takes hold of mine.

"I thought he was going to kill me. If it weren't for Buddy… God, poor Buddy. He saved me. We need to help him." I squeeze his hand hard, the tears flowing freely down my face.

He had to have some kind of connection to help him. I don't know much about motorcycle clubs, but the way Rhett walked around the jail like the king of the world, and the closet… Well, he has to know someone who can help me.

"Already ahead of you, darling. Buddy's going to be just fine."

His reassurance soothes, yet terrifies me at the same time. How can he make such a grand statement with so much confidence? Just how connected is their club? "How can you guarantee that?"

"Trust me. Buddy will want for nothing while he's on the inside. He took care of you, and we'll take care of him. Just glad he killed that bastard."

"Is Chad dead?" I whisper, like it's a secret. "Like, really dead?"

"As a fucking doornail."

"Rhett wanted… He was going to…" I start to tell him before the nurse returns. She takes one hard look at Judge and scowls.

"Who's this?"

"Uncle," he informs her.

She eyes him even more cautiously, like she's trying to figure out if he's lying or not. Apparently coming to a decision, she walks over and hands me two large pills in a paper cup. "Pain meds."

I release Judge's hand to take it from her and tip it back carefully. She hands me back the water cup, and I take a few sips before passing it back.

"Imaging should be here shortly," she informs me, all while watching Judge as she leaves the room.

"You don't need to worry about that shit, darling. Everything will be taken care of. Now, you get some rest. I'm going to go give your man an update before he tries to break down the doors of the jail. I'll be back in a bit."

He heads out of the room, leaving me with calming reassurance, but I have so many more questions. Rhett and I really need to talk.

STONEFACE

THE GUARD LEADS me into the courtroom for a second time, but this time, I see an angel smiling over at me from her place amongst my brothers in the MC.

I'm shuffled toward the defendant's table, but all I can do is stare at her gorgeous face, complete with a bruised cheek and black eye. It's been an entire week since I've seen her. Judge had kept me posted, and from the sounds of things, he and Delilah were developing quite the friendship.

I'm not ashamed to admit that makes me wild with jealousy. Not that I believe Delilah would ever sleep with Judge, or that Judge would even look at another woman other than his Grace. It's because he gets to spend time with her. He gets to see her outside of that fucking jail cell. He knows what she looks like in the sunshine.

When I reach my seat, the guard stumbles, not expecting me to keep walking. I don't go far, and he doesn't try to stop me.

Just a few steps past my table, I reach the waist-high wall that separates the spectators from the defendant. My hands are cuffed behind my back, but that's okay, because as soon as I get within reach, Delilah's hands dart out and grasp the sides of my face, pulling me to her and pressing her lips to mine.

"Your face," I say when we break apart.

"I'm fine," she assures me.

"If that fucker wasn't already dead, I'd kill him myself."

She kisses me again. "I'm fine."

"Miss Miller-Stewart, get your client to the table, please, or I'll have to hold him in contempt," the judge orders, sounding none too happy.

"Go, baby," Delilah whispers, sweeping the side of her nose against mine. The gesture is small and private, but somehow it feels monumental. It's making a statement to me and everyone else that she's mine.

"Mr. Darby, you need to sit," Brooke advises from behind me.

Leaning in, I press one last kiss to Delilah's lips and head for my seat. Everyone in the room has their eyes trained on me, but I couldn't care less. That moment with my woman had been fucking worth it.

"Mr. Darby," the judge begins as soon as the room grows silent. "I've needed the extra time to consider your case because to me, it wasn't so cut and dry. I've read your medical history, and the reports Miss Miller-Steward had presented about your military career." He cocks his brow. "However, as further evidenced by the men behind you, I think it's safe to assume you don't exactly live a totally law-abiding lifestyle. Am I correct in that assumption?"

I stare up at him, knowing this moment means something. I don't know what he's looking for here, but instead of feeding him some kind of horse shit lie, I tell him the truth. "That's correct, sir. We've had our share of run-ins with the law."

"But you still have no prior criminal record. Is that also correct?"

"Yes, sir." And it's true. I don't know how the fuck I've done the things I have without acquiring myself a record, but I've somehow managed to keep it clean.

"After reading over some of the files on your military career, I have to say, I thank you for your service and for the sacrifices you had to make in order to fulfill your role as a Marine for this country. Most men wouldn't have survived the things you have and still been able to function in society."

He doesn't know the half of it. I know my file is full of reports on the missions I'd been a part of, but I know it doesn't say word one about the pain I've had to endure witnessing the death and destruction I once had. It also doesn't say anything about nightmares I continue to have anytime I get even a whiff of a campfire, or the night sweats that rip me out of a solid sleep during a rainstorm.

"Thank you, sir."

"Considering all of that, along with the fact that Officer Dolan used excessive force, causing bodily harm to you upon booking, I've decided to sentence you with time served, plus one thousand hours of community service to be completed within five years' time. You will remain on probation for the next two years."

As he speaks, I hear whispered hoots of excitement from behind me. Though that same excitement is racing through my heart at this very moment, I don't react. "Thank you, sir."

"Mr. Rhett Darby," the judge says. "You're free to go." Lifting his gavel, he thumps it down onto the judge's bench. "Bailiff, clear the courtroom for the next case."

My entire being vibrates with excitement as the guard removes the metal chains around my ankles, and then my wrists.

"Thank you," I say, looking Brooke right in the eye. "You may look like Barbie, but in a courtroom, you're the scariest bitch I know."

Brooke grins. “Damn right.”

Once I’m free, I turn to my family behind the partition and nod before reaching out and grabbing Delilah around the waist and pulling her to me. “Time to collect on that treat you owe me.”

DELILAH

RHETT'S HAND grips mine tightly as we walk out of the courtroom, surrounded by half a dozen giant men in leather.

Leaning in so only he can hear me, I tell him, "Freedom looks good on you."

He gives my hand a gentle squeeze. "You look better."

We reach the bottom of the courthouse steps, and Rhett turns to face his buddies. "As much as I love you fuckers, I'll be doing my celebrating tonight with my Flower Child."

"You done doing dumbass shit?" the one with glasses asks him.

"Nope," he replies with a grin.

The man laughs and flips him off. "Good to have your moody ass back, brother."

Another man with an artfully arranged messy bun leans toward me and whispers, "You ever get tired of this big bastard, you come talk to me. I'll take care of you."

Rhett tugs me closer. "Fuck right off with that shit, TwatKnot, or I'll relocate that hair of yours directly into your rectum." Placing a kiss on my forehead, he warns, "Ignore that one."

"No woman can resist me," man bun jokes.

"Any woman with half a brain can," Judge quips, approaching us with Rhett's attorney at his side. She's so small next to him, but her confidence is bigger than him. Maybe it's the power suit, or the resting bitch face. All I know is that she had worked her magic in that courtroom. Rhett was fortunate to have her in his corner.

"I'd tell you all to stay out of trouble, but I'm doing some renovations on my house, so do your worst," she teases.

Judge reaches out to shake her hand. "Thank you. And tell your old man I said 'hello.'"

Smiling, she simply nods before turning and heading straight down the steps to a black town car parked at the curb. The driver, an older man, shuts the door behind her and returns to the driver's side before disappearing and pulling out into traffic.

Interesting.

"Do you guys do this often?" I'm genuinely curious.

"That's classified," the one with the glasses remarks, with the others getting a good chuckle out of it.

Rhett squeezes my hand harder. "If you assholes will excuse me, I would like to spend some time with my girl."

With a gentle tug, Rhett leads me away, and I turn back to give the others a quick wave.

"Wear a condom!" someone shouts.

Rhett shakes his head in clear annoyance, grumbling about assholes and murder weapons.

"Are they always like that?"

"This is mild for them. Just wait until we go to the clubhouse. They were on their best behavior here, but that shit goes out the window in our own place."

He stops at the edge of the street. Cars zip and zoom down the busy downtown road, but a break in the traffic finally comes so we can cross.

"Where's your car?" he asks when we reach the parking lot across from the courthouse.

I point straight at it, expecting him to keep walking, but instead, he stops dead in his tracks.

"The fuck is that thing?"

"That would be my car."

"That's a wind-up toy."

I frown. "No, it's a Prius, and his name is Barney."

"You named it?" Rhett barks out a laugh and shakes

his head. "I'm not going to fit in that thing, name or no name."

Releasing his hand, I dig out my keys and press the button to unlock the doors. "It's roomy inside." I open the passenger side door and point. "See?"

Rhett stares at me with unbridled skepticism, then leans down to peer inside. "Jesus," he mutters. "No videos of this shit."

He has to lower himself until he's practically on his knees to be able to pull his feet in. I stifle my grin as he contorts his body just enough to get his ass in the seat, but his knees are pressed into his chest. Reaching down between his legs, he finds the seat adjuster and manages to slide it back a few inches.

"You fit!" I declare.

Rhett glares up at me, and I can't hold back my laughter for another second. It hits me in gales of hilarity that cleanse my heart from all the crap we've been through since meeting one another. And even as I try to get myself under some sort of control, I look at him and see him folded up inside my little car, and it starts all over again.

"Just get in the car," he grumbles.

Walking around the back side, I let out a long, slow breath. It almost works too. For a second, I'm able to stop laughing. But then I pop open the door and slide into the driver's seat, noticing Rhett's enormous arm taking up half of it.

Another round of laughter washes over me, and this time, Rhett's laughing too.

"Is your place as small as this car?" he asks once we've settled down.

"Possibly," I tease.

"Let's Three Bears that shit and see if my Goldilocks ass fits in your bed."

"Awfully presumptuous of you to think that I'm going to invite you into my bed. I thought closets were your thing."

"As long as I get between those thick thighs of yours, Flower Child, it doesn't fucking matter where we are."

I flush. "Do you want to get something to eat first?"

"The only thing I need to eat is you, three times a day."

I gasp, my heart racing. "I, uh, guess we'll go to my place, then."

Putting the car in drive, we head off toward the highway. I merge into the traffic and head west toward the rescue. We ride in silence for a bit, but my mind keeps rolling through so many questions that I want to ask him about himself, the club, and how they can afford such a high-end attorney for his misdemeanor case. What exactly does his club do to have that kind of money?

"Can I ask you something about your club?"

"Depends on the question."

I mull over how to phrase what I want to ask him. "What do y'all do exactly? Like, do you go on charity rides or do bake sales?"

"Bake sales?" he snorts. "We're a brotherhood. We ride together and take care of business."

"That's a little vague."

He tries to shift in his seat to look at me, but he can't. "It's hard to explain to someone who hasn't lived our lifestyle."

"You're not going to scare me away."

He quietly considers that statement before speaking. "We aren't saints, Delilah. We've done some shit that most people wouldn't be able to accept, but we do it because we have to protect innocent people."

What he was planning to do to Chad, and his club's president's assurances about Buddy, click into place. They're the devils who do the devil's work. The necessary evils that protect us all.

"The club is always going to be a part of my life, but I need to know if that's something you can handle. There's going to be shit that I'm not going to be able to tell you, and you have to be okay with that."

"It's hard to wrap my head around the entire club thing," I admit hesitantly. "But they were there for you and for me. As long as you tell me what you can, I can handle it. I mean, I didn't grow up squeaky clean, either. Just wait until you meet my parents."

"Want me to meet the parents already?"

"It's only fair. I've met your family."

"Agreed. I think you'll like my club. You haven't even met the other old ladies yet. They'll love you."

"Old ladies?"

"It's what we call the women with our patched members. You'll get used to all that."

I laugh. "I may need a reference guide."

The rescue comes into view, and I turn onto the street that runs next to the building. Using the alleyway in the back, I pull up to my van behind the building.

He gapes out the window in shock. "You live in a fucking hippie van?"

"Mm-hmm," I say, proud of my cute little home. "It's got everything I could ever need." I climb out of the car and stand back, watching as Rhett carefully extracts himself from Barney.

I move to the back of the van and pop open the doors. My bed is made in the back, along with everything else I own. "Besides, it's just me here. What more could I need?"

Wide-eyed, Rhett takes it all in. "Is that a cat? And where's that bird's feathers?"

I point to the cage underneath the platform of my bed.

"Bunnies?" he asks, incredulous now.

"They were alone." I step inside, bending low to avoid hitting my head, and sit on the bed. "Now they have me."

Rhett's eyes burn with something that makes my belly do somersaults as I smile over at him. He watches me for a moment, not saying a word. Heat floods my cheeks as I feel the intensity rolling off of him in waves.

"What about me?" he asks after a few quiet moments.

I don't even recognize my own raspy voice when I say, "What about you?"

He puts his foot up, ready to climb inside with me. "Do I have you?"

I sink my teeth into my lower lip. "Yes."

"Do you want me?" He climbs onto the bed beside me, his face just inches from mine. His warm breath fans across my skin, sending the ripples in my belly into overdrive.

I hold his gaze, knowing this moment is pivotal for us, and place my hand on his cheek. "I want all of you."

His mouth covers mine as I finish those words, and this time is so much different from the last. This time, it's like two halves of a whole coming together. The meeting of two souls that have been separated for an eternity.

The first time we'd made love, it had been fast and hurried, filled with excitement at the prospect of being caught. But now we're in a bed. We have time to explore each other, and I can't wait to explore this beautiful man.

Reaching down, I grab his shirt and yank it up and over his head. His body hovers over mine, and I stare at the intricate tattoos that cover nearly every inch of his smooth skin.

"You'll have to tell me the stories behind of all of these," I murmur, kissing across his chest, my tongue dragging across his nipple as my fingernails glide gently down his back.

Groaning, he flops back on the bed, grabs my hips, and spins me so I'm sitting on top of him. "Not right now." Reaching up, he whips off my shirt.

"You're fucking beautiful, you know that?" he acknowledges, staring heatedly up at me.

Suddenly, I feel a little shy in just my jeans and bra, but he shuts me down fast. "Oh, no you don't. I want you to look in my eyes right fucking now."

My cheeks flare.

"Look at me," he coaxes.

Feeling like a total ass, I lift my eyes, looking at him from underneath my lashes.

"Now, repeat after me." His fingers trail up my arms until they reach my bra straps. "I." He slips the straps off of my shoulders, and a shiver races down my spine, hitting me right in my lower belly. "Say it, Flower Child."

Holding his stare, I do as I'm told. "I."

Bra straps now resting against my arms, Rhett traces his finger across my chest and down into the cup of my bra. When he grazes my nipple, I moan.

"Am." Tugging down on the cup, he exposes my breast to the cool evening air.

My pulse thrums beneath his touch. "Am."

Freeing my other breast, he continues. "The most beautiful woman."

The bed dips as he sits up, his lips just a whisper away from my breast. When he blows a steady stream of warm air across my nipple, I squirm, my need for him growing nearly out of control. "Say it, baby," he breathes.

I stare down at his lips just hovering there, willing him to take my breast into his mouth and touch me again. "Am the most beautiful woman."

Fucking hell, my center is aching now. I need him so badly.

"Rhett has ever seen." He finishes his sentence by flattening his tongue and dragging it across my sensitive bud before flicking wildly at it.

Gasping, I grind down against him, feeling his excitement through his jeans. "Rhett," I moan.

His teeth clamp down over my nipple. Holding it between his teeth, he asserts, "Say it, baby."

Hands on my thighs, my nipple still in his mouth, he thrusts his hips and grinds his erection against my center, pressing me down onto him until I fear I may explode. "Rhett has ever seen," I finish, barely able to breathe anymore.

His fingers drop to the button of my pants as he releases my breast. "Get your fucking pants off, Flower Child."

Doing exactly as I'm told, I roll to the side, pull my jeans off, and toss them away, with Rhett following suit. Hearing the crinkle of a condom wrapper, I turn in time to see him unravel the shiny disk of latex down over his impressive length.

Without a word, we both know what the other needs. Swinging my leg over top of him, I slide down slowly, taking him inside until I can't take any more.

He hisses as he stares down at where we're joined. "Fuckin' made for me," he mutters, rolling his hips, forcing himself deeper and dragging my clit over the well-manscaped patch of hair beneath it.

I'm not exactly a sex kitten, and I've not had a ton of partners, but I can tell you that when you're on the verge of orgasm, just from a man putting his beautiful cock inside you, you've got yourself a keeper.

And I'm going to keep him forever, if he'll let me.

That thought sets me off, and that's when I take over. Rhett's thumb hits my clit at just the perfect angle, and I move and roll and pump my hips, feeling every inch of him hit the most amazing places as I do it.

"Jesus Christ," he gasps, but I'm already gone.

Rainbows and fireworks explode inside of me, the colors fluttering with tiny tingles of pleasure. I keep moving, knowing that he's right there with me.

Rhett's fingers dig into my hips and he holds me tight, preventing me from moving, but I can't stop. It feels too fucking good.

I keep rocking, despite his protests, and our bodies quake in unison until neither one of us can move.

I drop down beside him and lay back on the mattress. His hand snakes out and grabs onto mine, pulling it to his chest to place it over his heart, which is racing out of control.

Chests heaving as we try to catch our breath, Rhett leans over and presses a kiss to my forehead. "A man could get used to this every day."

"Trust me," I say with a smile. "So could a woman."

He grows silent then, his eyes seeming distant.

"What are you thinking about?"

He shifts to pull me tight against him, and my body curves alongside his as I snuggle into him.

"How glad I am to be out, and how much I'm going to miss Penny. And how amazing you are, of course."

Kissing me again, he runs a finger across my lower lip before leaning back on the bed and drifting off to sleep. I lean into him and smile when a new rule pops into my head.

Rule Six. Everyone deserves to know real love.

THE SERIES

Dark Protector

Dark Secret

Dark Guardian

Dark Desires

Dark Destiny

Dark Redemption

Dark Salvation

STONEFACE

A SHOT GLASS lands on the counter in front of me, and Karma leans against the bar to my left. "Just wanted to say, respect for taking out that son of a bitch, Tucker. Wish I'd have done it myself, but if it couldn't be me, I'm glad it was you."

Henry Tucker's bullet had hit Karma in the heart, and he was damn lucky to be alive. "I'm happy to take on that stain for you and your girl. It had to happen, and now it's done."

Picking up our shot glasses, we clink them together, throw them back, and down the cold, burning tequila.

Leaning back, we watch the others having their beers while playing pool or darts. Leaning close, Karma advises, keeping his voice low, "You should've told us about your sister. It was bullshit we had to learn that in the courtroom."

I nod. "Guess I always kinda felt like Reba's story was mine. It kept her alive in a way, holding on to all that anger."

Karma stays silent.

"I fucked up!" I admit to everyone in the room. The voices fade as the men and women in the club drop what they're doing and give me their full attention.

"I should've told y'all about Reba, but she was my twin, ya know? It's been like a part of me died right along with her. How the fuck do you tell people you're only half a person?"

That question hangs heavy in the air, and nobody seems to have an answer. Finally, it's TwatKnot who breaks the silence. "Do you have any pics of your sister? Was she hot?"

Hashtag pounds his fist into TK's arm.

"What?" he cries. "It's just a question."

"Ignore him," Judge says, approaching from the far side of the room. "We get it. Your situation was tough, and I don't know that I'd have done anything different. Though I do know I wouldn't have walked away from my club."

I look down at my feet, feeling ashamed. That had been a stupid decision for sure.

"Regardless," Judge continues, "you're here now. Shit's been settled. Like I told you in that visitor's booth, we're a family. We have each other's backs, no matter what."

And that's when it all makes sense. When Elscher had done what he did to poor Reba, he had taken the only family I had. I made a second family of sorts while I was in the Marines, but one by one, I lost them, too.

When I'd joined the Black Hoods, it had been the lifestyle I'd been drawn to. I hadn't even noticed that along the way, they became as much of a family to me as Reba had been. All this time, I had been pissed off, seeking retribution and pushing away the club. It wasn't until now, letting that shit go, that I understand my family has been here all along. I just needed to shut the fuck up and notice them.

"Oh. And your friend, Buddy, is being taken care of as well."

My heart lurches. Poor Buddy. That big bastard had known so much pain in his young life. He would be dead within a week if they were to send him off to the state prison.

"They were getting ready to send him off to prison, but our mutual friend, Miss Brooke Miller-Stewart, put a stop to that real quick. Said his mental capacity makes that dangerous for him, and they're keeping him in solitary until his hearing. She says his original trial was a sham, with a public defender who didn't know shit. She thinks she can get him out, man."

Grinning, I slap Judge on the back. "You're a good fucking prez, ya know that?"

Judge chuckles. "Yeah, yeah. Don't thank me yet. Let's wait for blondie there to work her magic."

"Your attorney was hot, man. I'd steal a cop car if it meant spending time with her," TK chimes in, getting a laugh from the rest of the room.

"That's the only way she'd spend time with you," Karma quips from beside me.

That earns a roar of laughter.

I wait until the room settles down and ask, "How do you know her, anyway?"

"I've known that girl since she was just a wee little thing. Her old man did a lot of good for this club. We had an agreement, he and I. Now he's retired, and his little girl is a fucking shark in the courtroom. We're lucky to have her."

The door to the clubhouse opens, and my next question is cut off when I see Delilah walking toward me.

"What the fuck is that thing?" TK asks, pointing at her.

That's when I finally see her. Snuggled into Delilah's arms is my little Penny. As soon as she sees me, she lets out a yelp of excitement and squirms, wanting to be put down. Her nub of a tail wags, and finally, Delilah leans forward and places her on the floor."

Penny is on me in an instant. Dropping to the floor, I

grin as she climbs into my lap, showering me with kisses and her unconditional love.

"No, seriously. What is it?" TK repeats.

Delilah stands above us, a wide grin on her face as she observes our little reunion. "This is Rhett's dog. Her name is Penelope."

TK bursts into laughter. "You have a dog named Penelope? Do you put bows in her hair too?"

Glaring up at him from my place on the floor, I extend my middle finger, then go back to petting my dog.

"As a matter of fact—"

"Delilah," I bark, interrupting her before she tells him about my newly acquired expert dog bow skills.

Delilah claps her hand over her mouth and stifles a giggle, which sends TK over the edge.

Falling back in his chair, he throws his hand up and slams it down on the table. The rest of us can't help but join in as the two of them get a good laugh at my expense.

I run my fingers through Penny's hair. "I'm gonna teach you how to rip a grown man's balls off, okay?"

Penny opens her mouth, her eyes half-closed. Her heart is happy, and for the first time that I can remember in the last eighteen years, so is mine.

"Seriously, though," TK says as the room grows quiet once more. "Your sister. Was she hot?"

"She was beautiful," Delilah tells him. "Way out of your league."

That one gets a chuckle out of me. Delilah's been here two minutes, and has already learned to burn TK. She'll fit in just fine.

GP leans in and says, "Hot or not, your sister must've been a hell of a woman to survive in the womb with a big bastard like you."

I shoot another middle finger in the air, this one pointed at GP. But his joke doesn't bother me. Just the opposite, in fact. It feels good to talk about Reba. In a weird way, it almost feels like I have a part of her back again. She's not locked away inside me anymore.

And who better to share her with than Delilah, and this bunch of fuckers sitting here with me in this room.

TWATKNOT

LOOKING AROUND THE ROOM, I shake my head. Parties like this used to rage all night long. Booze and broads. Best fucking time of our lives, and a huge perk to being a member of this club is never running out of free pussy when I'm wearing this patch. It's literally a free-for-all. Shit, the only women in this room I've not had a go around with are the ones currently sidled up to their men, clutching their pearls. Don't get me wrong, I get it, but shacking up just ain't for me.

A few of my brothers start for the door, and I slam my beer down. "The fuck, guys?"

People turn their attention to me, and I feel like I'm the only one who hasn't officially lost my goddamn mind. "It's not even the last call, and y'all are sneaking out of here like you have an early day at work. The fuck happened to us? The night's still young."

"Night may be young, but I'm not," Mom mutters from beside me on the couch. "Been a shit year, man."

"No shit," Judge mutters.

Our club has been through hell and back this year, no doubt about it. Most of these fuckers have handed over their balls to a woman, and a few have had babies. Add on some good old-fashion cartels, dog fighting rings, and that shit with Henry Tucker, it's enough to drive any man over the edge.

I admit, it's been bad, but we're still here. We should be celebrating that shit.

"We need to do something, like fucking go somewhere!" I throw my arms out at my sides. "Let's celebrate the fact that we're still here and we're fucking alive."

"Your idea of celebrating and mine aren't really the same, TK," Karma declares.

"That's because I've pulled more strange than you, man. Don't be jealous."

Karma rolls his eyes. "You wouldn't know quality if it hit you in the balls."

"Quantity over quality, brother." I wink. "Seriously. Let's go fuck some shit up. Live a little."

"Dude, we've fucked up a bunch of shit," Burnt chimes in. "Like, a lot of shit."

I drag my hand over my face. Most of these guys have families and shit now, but we've been missing a key thing that makes our club a club, and that's fucking fun, and all that brotherhood shit.

"That's not what I'm talking about. We need to hit the open road and just go somewhere. No drama. No fighting." I pause. "Isn't Sturgis coming up?"

Sturgis Motorcycle Rally used to be a yearly thing for our club. Our vacation, or whatever the fuck the white picket fence families did together. Ten days of a good fucking time with booze and all the free pussy a man could want. The latter being my favorite part of the trip, of course. It's one thing to pull a little local strange, but sampling what Sturgis has to offer? There's nothing else like it. With these fuckers all settling down, it just means more fun for me.

"What's Sturgis?" Priest asks.

I shove off the couch and point at him. "That shit right there. A patch should know what Sturgis is. This is bullshit, guys. We're doing this man and his cock a disservice. We need to take our shit and put some rubber on the road."

Grace walks in with a few of the other ladies in tow from the back rooms. She sidles up to Judge, and he wraps his arm around her shoulders. "What's going on?"

"He thinks we need to go to Sturgis for the rally."

"Rally?" Grace arches her brow at Judge. "What's that?"

"See? Y'all keep making my point for me." I drag my hand over my beard. "Let's do this."

"It's a bike week up in South Dakota," Judge explains to Grace. The president's old lady should know shit like this. Hell, she barely knows the basics. She and all the other ladies should get to experience MC life from more seasoned biker bitches. This trip could solve a lot of shit for us all.

"It's more than that," I say, grabbing a beer and hoisting it in the air. "Sturgis is brotherhood. Togetherness. It's motorcycles and booze. Music and quality Kush. And better fucking pussy."

"Is that all you think about?" Grace shakes her head. "One of these days, being a man whore is going to bite you in the ass."

"Doubt that, sweetheart. Good looking guy like me? It's just how I'm wired. Ya know, alpha male and all that."

"More like an arrogant asshole," she mutters, which makes Judge chuckle.

I ignore them and address the rest of the room. "What do you say, assholes? Sturgis? Let's do this shit."

"Man, I don't know," GP pipes up. "Blair's about to pop. I can't just drop shit and go, man."

"Do you hear yourself right now? When the fuck did we all turn into a bunch of pussies?"

'Bout the time they all decided to family up, I think, but I refrain from saying that out loud with the ladies present.

I look around the room at my brothers. None of these fuckers say a goddamn word. "Guys, come on, it's ten days. What's the worst that could happen?"

Judge looks over at Grace, who simply nods. Shrugging those big fucking shoulders of his, he hollers, "Fuck it! Let's do it!"

"Oh, fuck yeah!" I shout, then down what's left of my beer.

Look out, Sturgis. Daddy's coming home.

Read more about TwatKnot's story in Dark Redemption.

THE SERIES

Dark Protector

Dark Secret

Dark Guardian

Dark Desires

Dark Destiny

Dark Redemption

Dark Salvation

Dark Seduction

Avelyn Paige is a USA Today and Wall Street Journal bestselling author who writes stories about dirty alpha males and the brave women who love them. She resides in a small town in Indiana with her husband and three fuzzy kids, Jezebel, Cleo, and Asa.

Avelyn spends her days working as a cancer research scientist and her nights sipping moonshine while writing. You can often find her curled up with a good book surrounded by her pets or watching one of her favorite superhero movies for the billionth time. Deadpool is currently her favorite.

Want to talk books? Join Avelyn's Facebook group to learn about new releases, future series, and to hang out with other readers.

ALSO BY AVELYN PAIGE

The Heaven's Rejects MC Series

Heaven Sent

Angels and Ashes

Sins of the Father

Absolution

Lies and Illusions

The Dirty Bitches MC Series

Dirty Bitches MC #1

Dirty Bitches MC #2

Dirty Bitches MC #3

Other Books by Avelyn Paige

Girl in a Country Song

Cassie's Court

Geri Glenn writes alpha males. She is a USA Today Bestselling Author, best known for writing motorcycle romance, including the Kings of Korruption MC series. She lives in the Thousand Islands with her two young girls, one big dog and one terrier that thinks he's a Doberman, a hamster, and two guinea pigs whose names she can never remember.

Before she began writing contemporary romance, Geri worked at several different occupations. She's been a pharmacy assistant, a 911 dispatcher, and a caregiver in a nursing home. She can say without a doubt though, that her favorite job is the one she does now–writing romance that leaves an impact.

Want to talk books? Join Geri's Facebook group to learn about new releases, future series, and to hang out with other readers.

ALSO BY GERI GLENN

The Kings of Korruption MC series.

Ryker

Tease

Daniel

Jase

Reaper

Bosco

Korrupted Novellas:

Corrupted Angels

Reinventing Holly

Other Books by Geri Glenn

Dirty Deeds (Satan's Wrath MC)

Hood Rat

Printed in Great Britain
by Amazon